20173022

Books by Alice Leader

POWER AND STONE
SHIELD OF FIRE

ALICE LEADER

SHIELD OF FIRE

PUFFIN

PUFFIN BOOKS

Published by the Penguin Group
Penguin Books Ltd, 80 Strand, London WC2R 0RL, England
Penguin Group (USA), Inc., 375 Hudson Street, New York, New York 10014, USA
Penguin Books Australia Ltd, 250 Camberwell Road, Camberwell, Victoria 3124, Australia
Penguin Books Canada Ltd, 10 Alcorn Avenue, Toronto, Ontario, Canada M4V 3B2
Penguin Books India (P) Ltd, 11 Community Centre, Panchsheel Park, New Delhi – 110 017, India
Penguin Group (NZ), cnr Airborne and Rosedale Roads, Albany, Auckland 1310, New Zealand
Penguin Books (South Africa) (Pty) Ltd, 24 Sturdee Avenue, Rosebank 2196, South Africa

Penguin Books Ltd, Registered Offices: 80 Strand, London WC2R 0RL, England

www.penguin.com

First published 2004
1

Copyright © Alice Leader, 2004
All rights reserved

The moral right of the author has been asserted

Set in 12.25/16 pt Monotype Garamond
Typeset by Rowland Phototypesetting Ltd, Bury St Edmunds, Suffolk

Made and printed in England by Clays Ltd, St Ives plc

British Library Cataloguing in Publication Data
A CIP catalogue record for this book is available from the British Library

ISBN 0–141–31528–8

To Roz Leader

. . . It is impossible to deny that a shield was used to make a signal, because that actually happened, but I can add nothing beyond what I have already said on the matter of who the signaller was.

Herodotus
The Histories, Book VI [124]

ACKNOWLEDGEMENTS

The principal source for the historical events depicted in the novel is Herodotus, *The Histories*, Books V and VI. Among the most helpful of the books I have consulted about the life of Athenian girls and women *c.*490 BC are *The Athenian Woman: An Iconographic Handbook*, by Sian Lewis; *Pandora: Women in Classical Greece*, by Ellen D. Reeder; *Courtesans and Fishcakes: the Consuming Passions of Classical Greece*, by James Davidson.

I am indebted to A. Trevor Hodge, Distinguished Research Professor of Classics, Carlton Universitry, Ottawa, for his invaluable help, corrections and encouragement on all matters, but especially on the issue of the shield raised up at the Battle of Marathon. On-site research in Santorini (Thira in the novel) and in Athens was greatly facilitated by Emmanuela de Nora. I am obliged to Effie Tsomlectsoglou and to Fifi G. Vervelidis for their advice and introductions on Santorini, and to Robert and Mary Kylie for their suggestions in Athens.

Others to whom I am particularly grateful for help of several sorts are Joan Dyer-Westacott, of the American School in London, and Roz and Zachary Leader, who read drafts for me, pointing out missed connections and suggesting areas for clarification. Any errors contained in *Shield of Fire* are, of course, my own.

Alice Leader

CONTENTS

VI TROPHE AND NIKE: 490 BC, LATE SUMMER

GREECE 490 BC

AEGEAN SEA

MEDITERRANEAN SEA

MILETUS

DELOS

MARATHON

ATHENS

AEGINA

DELPHI

SPARTA

THIRA

SEA OF CRETE

CRETE

IONIAN SEA

100 km

100 Miles

I

Persephone was running along the sloped fields, laughing with her friends. They had gone to pick flowers. Persephone wanted to find the perfect bloom, the one that was the tallest, opened the widest, and was of the deepest scarlet. She looked and looked, running this way and that. Then she saw the head of a most wonderful poppy. Persephone could not resist and ran to reach and pluck it.

Each footfall the running girls took resounded in the cavern above the head of Hades, god of the Underworld. Their laughter was faint, but the beating of their sandals drew his attention. He never knew what was happening in the world above unless someone struck the ground or called to him in oaths or curses. The tapping and slipping and sliding of the girls' sandals made him smile. He glanced up, through the earth's crust, to see one set of sandals running apart from the others. He looked more closely at the silky feet: the kitten-soft toes, like just-boiled shrimp, tiny, pink, curling. Then Hades lifted his eyes to the girl's face. She was the most beautiful creature he had ever seen. He had to have her.

Up through the earth the black chariot of Hades stormed, cleaving the crust and forcing a gap in the ground. Those who saw it could not believe their eyes. Nor would they ever forget the sound of the heavy thud of the horses' hooves as the chariot rounded on the stricken girl.

CATASTROPHE

492 BC

1. NIGHTMARE

Nyresa cried out in her sleep. The whole earth shook and she felt herself sliding towards the huge hole in the middle of the kitchen. Everything around her was falling, tumbling – jars, chairs, crockery. A persistent rumbling tore through the house, and the stone staircase to her bedroom snapped in two. She kept slipping, sliding towards the deep break in the earth. She couldn't breathe. The hot air, full of ash, coated her mouth and blocked her throat. Her eyes burned, as if shrivelling in the heat. Then she began to fall: down, down into the fissured earth, rocks and boulders crashing round her, down to the black Underworld.

'Nyresa. Nyresa. Wake. Wake, my darling,' her grandmother crooned, shaking her gently, smoothing her hair back from her forehead. The grandmother's old, soft hand was covered with brown age spots. Her thickened fingers, gripped by rings long grown too tight, soothed the child.

'Are you dreaming of the earthquake again?' Her own forehead was creased in worry; she looked down tenderly at the little girl. The island's history of earthquakes, tidal waves and volcanic eruptions filled Nyresa's dreams.

Nyresa opened her eyes and stared into the darkness. She nodded, brimming tears about to spill.

'Shush,' the grandmother said as she continued to stroke her granddaughter's forehead. 'Hades did not take you. Look, you're right here – in your bed. As for earthquakes, all of that was so long ago it has become a bedtime story for children.'

In a storyteller's rocking rhythm, the grandmother whispered, 'Long ago, very long ago, the ground of Thira shook, rumbling and cracking. Giants, buried deep under the earth, tossed and turned. One day the mountain right in the centre of the island blew high into the sky – and vanished.' With a gentle smile the grandmother continued, 'And where the mountain used to be, we have the beautiful caldera, filled with lovely, warm blue water. Beneath it all, the giants sleep calmly.'

Nyresa listened, mesmerized as ever, her eyes looking inwards, remembering the stories her grandmother had told her. She thought of Persephone and her mother, Demeter, goddess of fertility. Every Greek girl was raised on their story. 'One day the giants will awake again,' Nyresa whispered.

Her grandmother raised her eyebrows and nodded her head to the side. 'Yes, perhaps. That is why we pray to the gods, my darling.'

'But in my dream, Grandmother, the ground gapes and I fall into it, deep down under the earth, and no one can hear me or save me. Hades has me. My mother doesn't come to save me.'

'Enough!' The grandmother was now stern. The nightmares concerned her. Though the child was twelve, she was filled with fears. The grandmother gently rocked Nyresa while she thought. Then to Nyresa she spoke quietly. 'In two weeks the whole island honours the gods. You and I will make a special prayer to Artemis, protector of maidens. Now, hush.' She bent her head to kiss the crying girl.

Nyresa fell asleep in her grandmother's arms. Her grandmother looked down at the pale, troubled face and shook her head in dismay. I must pray, too, to Demeter for help with this child, she thought.

2. CALDERA

When Nyresa woke in the morning, she wanted to be alone. She slipped out of the house on to the stone streets of Thira. As always, she looked to her left, to the sea. Hers was the last of a row of stone houses – in a honeycomb of stone houses. Thira was built on top of a marble mountain and, although it was not very big, it was complex and crowded, with houses curled between houses and walls so high they cut out the sun, turning streets into tunnels.

The bright-blue waters gleamed some fifteen hundred steps below. The city was perched on the very top of the highest and most southerly of the island's mountains. The ancient people – the Spartans, who long ago controlled the Minoan trade routes and Thira – used to call the island

Stronghili, the circular isle, or Kalliste, the fairest isle. Now Nyresa's city and the island were both called Thira. To Nyresa, the island below looked like the crescent moon, or a happy person opening her arms welcomingly to the west. She smiled. No one can see our city, from the sea or the beach or from the fields surrounding the mountain's base, she thought. But I can see forever.

She turned south and curled south-west to the temple of Apollo, the most ancient of Thira's temples, perched on the tip of the mountain plateau, overlooking the sea. Though roofed, the temple had only three walls, the west side being open to the sea. She walked past the temple, past the columns, each carved with a ram's head, with long, curved horns wrapping back round the column, and bunches of stone grapes hanging over the rams' eyes and festooning their horns.

Now the top of the cliff was right before her. And beyond that, infinite blue sky and endless blue water. Her eyes could not see all the blue, for it surrounded her. Birds, specks of dark against the sky and sea, circled far below. The wind blew all about her, making her feel like one of the birds swirling against the blue. Nyresa walked to the very tip of the temple's platform, sat on the cliff's edge, and dangled her feet over the steep drop. Directly below lay the Sea of Crete, then, to her left and right as far as the eye could see, gleamed the Aegean.

She scanned the horizon. Tiny ships dotted the seascape, leaving pretty white wave plumes in their wake. The only sound that penetrated the whirring wind was the bleating of sheep, the occasional mooing of cows – and one tardy cockerel. Certainly no sound could be heard of the waves below or of the farmers on the terraces and the plains calling to each other. She sighed and swung her legs, knocking the heels of her sandals against the rock face. Memories of her nightmare slipped away from her.

She'd been sitting alone for a while when her friend Glyka's voice broke into her thoughts. 'There you are, Nyresa. I'm glad I found you. There's a big meeting in the Agora and everyone's shouting. A boatload of people just arrived from an island east of us. They say the Persians are attacking all the islands and cities along the Ionian coast!'

'Are we in danger?' Nyresa asked quickly. Glyka was practical and clever and Nyresa trusted her views. Her parents were very protective and their cautious attitudes, repeated by Glyka, were usually reliable.

Glyka sat down beside Nyresa. Just by the way she settled on to the cliff edge Nyresa was reassured. 'No,' Glyka replied. 'I think we're far enough away.' The two girls gazed out into the blue. 'Nyresa,' Glyka began in a thoughtful voice, 'I've been thinking about the Persians.'

Nyresa glanced sideways at her friend. She liked Glyka's matter-of-fact way. Glyka means 'sweet', and sweet Glyka was. But what soothed Nyresa was Glyka's way of looking right into whatever frightened her. As for Glyka, what she liked about Nyresa was her loyalty and her seriousness. Nyresa had never known her mother, who died giving birth to her, and had hardly known her father, who had died at sea. Orphaned at an early age, she lived alone with her grandmother, Epiktiti, the priestess. The two girls had been friends since they were small and shared their most private thoughts.

'You know how anxious my parents are about me,' Glyka began. 'They've been talking a lot at home about this war with Persia, trying to decide if we are in danger.' The two girls gazed out to sea, swinging their feet. They both knew the Persians and Greeks had been battling along the Ionian coast for seven years.

Nyresa frowned. 'But the Persians don't care about Thira, do they? Our island is far outside their empire.' She didn't like to think of the huge Persian empire now targeting tiny Thira.

Glyka shrugged her shoulders. 'My parents say the Persian emperor, Darius, has decided to wipe out all Greek resistance – not just from those Ionian Greeks he's already conquered, but all Greeks everywhere.' She turned to look at Nyresa. 'They say he'll take Athens, then Sparta, then all the lands and islands.'

'Why?' Nyresa was scared and outraged at once.

Glyka looked again over the sea. 'They say he's angry at Athens and plans to destroy it – then use those same forces to conquer all other Greek cities and make them part of his empire.'

'So he's angry at Athens because they've sent ships and soldiers to help the Ionians?'

Glyka nodded. 'And he wants a former dictator of Athens, Hippias, to be welcomed back and allowed to rule again as dictator.' Glyka smiled at her friend. 'Don't ask me

– I don't know why. But the emperor Darius is furious the Athenians won't take back Hippias.'

Nyresa knew why. 'My grandmother says the Athenians rule themselves now and like it that way.' The Revolt had happened when she and Glyka were only five but she had often heard adults talking about Darius's anger. In Thira the big landowners ruled, but everyone else seemed to have a say – and were probably having that say right now in the Agora.

'Those don't seem very good reasons to *me* for attacking Thira,' Glyka said, shaking her head. 'Let Darius attack Athens if he wants, but leave *us* alone.'

Nyresa grew quiet. Her eyes followed ships criss-crossing the sea. Some were heading south, perhaps to Crete or Egypt or maybe to Phoenicia. Some were headed north to the islands in the Aegean, maybe on to Athens, or even further north, to the top of the Aegean. Nyresa remembered what her grandmother had told her: Thira had always been valued for its location. It lay in the centre of all sea routes, whether for trade or conquest. Thira might well be extremely useful to the Persians.

'What happens if the Persians attack?' Nyresa asked.

'My parents told me that first they ask for "earth and water",' Glyka replied, 'which means total submission. If those they have conquered agree, they are spared and become part of the empire. If they don't, they are attacked. All the men and boys are killed, along with the old and the weak. The women and girls are enslaved, and sent to other parts of the empire.' Glyka and Nyresa exchanged looks.

9

'Will Thira give earth and water, if it is attacked?' Nyresa asked.

'That's what they're talking about now in the Agora, Nyresa,' Glyka replied quietly.

Nyresa knew her grandmother would be there. Epiktiti was the head priestess to Artemis and very important. The gods Artemis and Apollo, sister and brother, had always been worshipped as the main protectors of Thira. 'Does anyone think Thira has to decide soon?' she asked her friend.

'No,' Glyka said, 'certainly not this summer. The Persian fleet is headed north up the Ionian coast, away from us.'

Nyresa's face brightened into a grin. 'Then let's go sailing today, Glyka! Let's get away from all the talk.'

Glyka grinned back at her. 'Why not? My uncle told me he's skipping the meeting in the Agora, doesn't want to go. Instead he's taking his boat out today into the caldera. Shall we go?'

Nyresa's face darkened.

Glyka watched her carefully. Somehow the caldera and earthquakes and her mother's death were linked for Nyresa, Glyka knew, though she could never understand how. Nyresa's mother had died giving birth to her. This had nothing to do with earthquakes or volcanoes. Soon after, her father had drowned at sea, sailing to Cyrene, one of Thira's colonies.

'All right,' Nyresa said, screwing up her courage. 'Let's go.'

The two girls jumped up and ran back to the city. There

were two main streets in Thira, one straight through the Agora and lined on both sides by houses, and one just to its north. The girls chose the northern street. Nyresa figured she could slip off for a few hours without permission, as Epiktiti would be occupied by the public debate.

The girls hopped and trotted like little goats down the mountain. It was wonderful, scampering down the dirt path, with the plain suddenly appearing, growing larger and larger. Nyresa and Glyka had sprinted down this path hundreds of times and, no matter how steep, never needed to look down to find their footing. This mountaintop and these plains were their world. They refused to think about the future.

When they got to the bottom they shot along the wheat and barley fields, waving at the farmers. The crops were planted right up to the narrow beach, with its black, volcanic sand and slate-grey water. The girls stood on the black sand and stared up at their mountain. It was impossible to see even a single building of Thira from the shore. Safe from pirates or Persians, Nyresa thought happily.

Glyka, with Nyresa just behind, saw her uncle and began waving to him. She ran up to him as he stood near the simple skiff he used for fishing. Nyresa saw him nod enthusiastically. The girls helped him push the boat off the beach, into the water. The boat had one sail and two oars, with three wooden seats across the width. Just before the girls climbed in, each touched the sea, then her forehead and heart, and offered a little prayer of thanks and a request for safekeeping to Poseidon. Nyresa looked up at the sun and silently spoke to Artemis: please stop my nightmares and protect us, Artemis, from the Persians.

They sailed west, around the beach that eventually curved into the caldera. Soon they were out of sight of the city as they kept circling the island to the north-west. The day was beautiful, sunny and clear, the water a shimmering blue-green. The beach pressed up against a bank of volcanic ash, three fathoms deep. The ash, over a thousand years old, was wind-carved in swirls, tunnels, holes and honeycombs.

'Those cliffs look like my grandmother's wheat cakes when we cook them on the griddle and their tops bubble up,' Nyresa observed.

Just then Nyresa saw something big leap out of the water near them. 'Glyka! Look!' Off the starboard side of the boat a school of dolphins was racing them, arching, snorting, diving. There must have been ten, twelve. The girls watched as they flew along in the water, and saw their beady eyes and funny sideways smiles. Then, as suddenly as they had come, they disappeared, turning abruptly to the south towards Crete.

The two girls looked at each other. They knew the god Poseidon, Lord of the Seas, rode the waves with a company of dolphins. Had Poseidon honoured them with his presence? Glyka's uncle, who often saw dolphins, put great store by them. He looked at the girls and winked. Then he sat back in silence as their boat gracefully slid into the bottomless caldera.

Nyresa's eyes swept around the circle of brown and red land, covered with its white ash mantle. Perhaps I'm afraid of the caldera because the water here is so strange, she thought. It isn't like the sea, with waves, or a river. It is still. Yet it flows in and out between the islands that enclose the caldera. It is so deep no ship's anchor can find bottom. Perhaps there is no seabed, she thought, only a direct passage to the Underworld.

The girls stared at the surrounding land as the little boat sailed on. 'Now these cliffs look like pastry,' Glyka said, breaking the silence. 'My mother makes a very sweet layered pastry with honey and crushed nuts in between.' Nyresa shrugged her shoulders, looking glum. Her mood had clearly changed as they entered the caldera.

'Here we are,' Glyka's uncle announced, 'smack in the middle of the caldera, right over the top of the volcano! Look down and see the bubbles, the yellow water. Put your hand in and feel how warm it is.' He smiled cheerfully at them. 'Don't wake the sleeping giants, girls!' he joked. Glyka threw him a happy glance. On one side of their boat the sea was yellow, on the other, azure blue!

He didn't see Nyresa's reaction as she had bent her face over the edge of the boat. An underground stream of yellow water rose up in the midst of deepest blue. Bubbles surrounded the boat and the sea smelled of rotten eggs. Her eyes sought the blurry outline where the yellow and blue waters mingled. She was ashen.

Glyka's uncle looked at the silent girl and frowned. 'Nyresa, nothing to be afraid of here. Look, see, off the other side of the boat, the little fishes? Thousands of them!'

The girls raised their heads and looked the other way, into the azure sea, and were delighted by clouds of silver flashes turning this way and that, deep into the blue.

'They love being near this hot water. Feel it, I tell you!' Glyka's uncle leaned over the side and trailed his fingers in the bubbling water. Glyka gently dipped her fingers, hoping not to scare away the silver flashes, and eventually, slowly, Nyresa did the same. 'The sea here is as warm as water in a cooking cauldron,' the uncle pronounced, 'just before it gets really hot. Away from this warm patch there are big fish, but nothing to worry about. I'd love to catch some of those huge tuna or a nice big octopus.'

Nyresa did not answer: instead she laid her head on her arm along the boat's rim, pretending to look over the side into the water. But she was really looking into her own mind, remembering her nightmares – the earthquake, the roaring sounds, the gaping hole and Hades standing there. Then she looked down at the bubbling water, impossible to see through. Where did the bubbles go? She reached out again towards the water. From the centre of the earth, from the Underworld, these bubbles come up to my hand, then disappear, she thought. She tried to look again deep into her own heart, into her fears, to see what lay beneath them. Like the yellow water, all was murky.

Glyka and her uncle caught Nyresa's mood. As the boat headed back to the ash-cliff beach and its mooring on the plain below Thira, Glyka's uncle could no longer suppress his anxieties. Glyka saw his worried expression – but she could think about the future only for a moment, it scared her so. If the Persians take our lovely island, they will . . . she cut off her thoughts.

In silence the three sailed home, arriving at the familiar plain on which farmers and their families harvested crops, getting ready for the feast of Apollo and Artemis. All three whispered prayers to Apollo and Artemis – and, not forgetting the leaping dolphins, to Poseidon.

The girls climbed the mountainside together and then separated, planning to meet again tomorrow as usual.

As Nyresa walked along the southern street, she saw the Agora emptying of people and knew the meeting was over. She sensed the adults' mood was solemn but not alarmed. But when she saw her grandmother coming towards her, her stomach knotted. Everything about Epiktiti's expression scared Nyresa.

3. KORE

'Come, my darling. I need to speak to you. Shall we go for a walk?'

Nyresa looked deeply into her grandmother's eyes, but was denied entry: this was a serious talk to be held in private. Nyresa nodded. In unison they crossed the Agora and climbed the stone steps to the upper level of the city. Walking north along the narrow top of the mountain, they soon came to the steep but grassy slope on their left that ran down to the island's western plain. Being on top of the mountain Nyresa felt like an eagle poised to swoop down and circle lazily over the vast, blue sea. The sun and the winds seemed to be competing to show who was the stronger. Worried as she was, Nyresa couldn't help but wonder who would win today, Apollo the sun god or Aeolus, god of the winds.

She looked down the slope. Again she saw the beautiful army of stone statues, standing life-size, guarding the dead. She loved these statues. There were statues of young men, of young women, all beautiful; several stood two metres high. Of course most people couldn't afford to erect such splendid monuments over their dead and had, instead, stone markers or smaller stone figures or jars. But down the slope more than twenty tall statues stood guard.

Nyresa's favourite was near her mother's grave. This kore, as the young woman statues were called, was not her mother's guard, but Nyresa liked to pretend she was. In fact, the kore had stood there more than a hundred years before her mother had died. She was different from all the other kores, for she did not smile. Most people, Nyresa knew, loved the gentle, welcoming smile these stone guardians wore. The sweet smiles reassured them that death was not terrible and might even be familiar and comfortable. What Nyresa loved was her kore's solemnity. One should not smile at death, she thought. Death takes people away and leaves others lonely.

Her kore had eyes that looked straight ahead, lips simply closed, not compressed and certainly not smiling. Her face was beautiful, serene and without lines. She had beads in her hair and a ribbon around her head, held just above her ears and tied in a bow at the back. Her hair was long, braided just at the ends, and reached past her shoulders. One arm was against her side. The other was crossed over her heart. She had the most beautiful, slender figure Nyresa had ever seen; it was completely lifelike yet absolutely perfect. She was wearing a round-neck tunic and a skirt, delicately gathered in the front with two pleats, but fuller in the back with eight pleats. At the top of the skirt was a wide buckled belt, tightly encircling her tiny waist.

Nyresa and her grandmother reached her kore. While her grandmother slowly lowered herself on to a large flat rock, her strong, old hands gripping the rock's sides, Nyresa sank to the ground, pressing her back against the back of the kore's skirt. No matter what her grandmother had in mind to say, Nyresa now felt safe. She gazed over the vast drop to the plain below and over the endless water. The wind whirled about her head, but she felt the warmth of the kore's stone skirt and the comfort of sitting, not moving. Her grandmother watched her.

'Nyresa?' Nyresa turned to face her grandmother. 'I didn't see you at the meeting. I wondered where you were and how you are. Did your nightmare come back to you today?'

'I went sailing with Glyka and her uncle. We sailed into the centre of the caldera,' Nyresa answered.

'Do you know what the meeting was about?'

Nyresa nodded. 'Glyka told me.'

They sat in silence for a while, the strong wind blowing about them. The grandmother's white hair, still thick, was held back by a length of cloth tied about her head. Nyresa's black curls flew about. Her bright red tunic, belted at the waist, stood out dramatically against the sun-bleached brown grass, the grey marble rocks, white tombstones and sculpted grave guardians. Epiktiti wore black, out of respect for her dead and in keeping with her august position as head priestess of Artemis.

'Nyresa, I want to go on a pilgrimage.'

Nyresa looked up at her grandmother.

'There are two important matters on my mind. One is what our gods wish for us and the other is your nightmares.'

'But I'm fine. The nightmares aren't so bad!' Nyresa quickly answered.

'Listen to me,' her grandmother commanded. 'We heard today that the Persian fleet has sailed out of the Persian mainland and up into the Aegean Sea. Mardonius is their commander. The boat people believe he is sailing north, along the Ionian coast. At the moment we do not have to worry.' She looked off into the sea and then back at Nyresa. 'I need to pray to our gods to find out what we should do. If we are invaded, could we live – would our gods allow us to live – under Darius's rule, and the rule of his god, Ahura-Mazda? Would Zeus, Athena, Apollo, Artemis, Poseidon, all our gods, give their blessings to such an accommodation? I cannot imagine Darius conquering the Greek lands without our gods' consent. Yet the Persians are advancing.'

After a pause Epiktiti continued. 'Seven years ago I watched the Ionian Revolt, and two years ago saw how Darius crushed it. He has conquered his rebellions and is looking for more land. Nyresa, the Persians are not coming to Thira now, but I do believe Darius has plans for future conquest. We need guidance. I want to go to Athens, to pray to Athena and Artemis on the Acropolis. I want to go to Brauron where Artemis is especially honoured and Crete where, they say, Artemis chose her young girl attendants. And I will go to Delos, where Apollo and Artemis were born. I am the head priestess of Artemis here. It is my duty to interpret the gods and lead our people accordingly.'

'Will I go with you? When will we return?' Nyresa felt dizzy with the enormity of these questions.

Epiktiti did not reply but continued gently, 'There is another reason I must go – and it's you, Nyresa. Your dreams trouble me. I had hoped as you grew older these nightmares would stop, but they haven't. I think that the gods might be trying to tell us something about you. I don't understand what that might be. I have decided to consult Demeter, to ask her for help. Demeter is the eternal mother who understands loss. Your nightmare echoes the experience of Demeter's daughter, Persephone, who was stolen by Hades to live with him in the Underworld. I will go to Demeter's shrine in Athens and to Eleusis where her sacred temple is. In a month's time, the annual gathering of pilgrims takes place. I must be there. I will pray to her, Nyresa, and to her life-giving daughter, Persephone. I will pray for guidance.'

Although she heard these words, all Nyresa could say was, 'Am *I* going with you, Grandmother? Will you leave me here alone on Thira?'

Epiktiti smiled encouragingly. 'I won't leave you here. But you cannot accompany me on my pilgrimage. We have relatives in Athens, your father's brother, his wife, and their daughter. You will live with them. I will be gone some time and am unlikely to be able to send you messages. I will leave some money with your uncle to cover your expenses and allow you some spending money. In time, I expect us to return to Thira.'

Nyresa's mind reeled. The rocks and statues and stone markers around her began to swirl. But she had to speak, she had to regain control. 'Grandmother, why Athens? How can I be safe in Athens? Glyka says Darius hates Athens and is coming to attack it!'

Her grandmother nodded, as much to herself as to Nyresa. 'Of course I have thought of this. Athens is well defended. The Persians are unlikely to attack and destroy Athens, but if they do, all Greek cities and islands will come under Persian control. You would not be safer elsewhere. Thira would not be safer, Nyresa. If Athens falls, no Greek city is safe.'

'But what does "in time" mean, Grandmother? How long will we be apart? The Persians could attack Athens or Thira before you return.'

'They could, but I do not believe they will. What you must remember, Nyresa, is that nothing happens on earth without our gods' consent. We must trust our gods. If they want Darius to take Athens, he will. But I need to understand what *we* can do in response.'

Nyresa stared at her grandmother and then gave a

crooked, brave smile. '"In time" could be a long time and I will miss you.'

Epiktiti smiled back. 'I'll miss you, too. But you will like Athens and, I think, your cousin. She is very beautiful and everyone speaks well of her. Her name is Rhode and she is fifteen, three years older than you. She is crippled, Nyresa, and will be grateful for your company.'

Suddenly everything was too much. Nyresa felt dizzy. She began to fall . . . down into the fissured earth, down to the black Underworld. As she slumped into unconsciousness at the feet of her kore she was aware of someone crying out to her.

4. CYRENE

Nyresa awoke the next morning disorientated and sad. She had no recollection of being carried by worried Thirans to her home. Hazily she remembered being soothed by her grandmother and put to bed. Glyka had once told Nyresa she liked her seriousness. Today Nyresa felt very serious.

I must be more like Glyka, she told herself. I must shake myself, get up, and fly into the face of whatever is bothering me. I must be more practical and brave. She jumped out of bed, dressed, and went down the stone stairs to find her grandmother's servant, Thratta. Perhaps I can help her in the kitchen, she thought.

Thratta had already milked the goat and was now standing at the stone basin in the middle of the room, straining curds through muslin. Dough was rising in a covered bowl set by the hearth. A pot containing a meat stew hung over the glowing fire. Nyresa smiled to think how her grandmother cooked meat; as if to remind anyone who smelled it that she, a priestess – unlike others – did not have to wait for sacrifice, for the male priest to sanctify and distribute her portion.

'May I help you with anything in the kitchen, Thratta?' Nyresa asked, determined to be cheerful.

Thratta looked up, pleased. She knew about Nyresa's nightmares and handled the girl gently, not embarrassing her by talking about them while still always being kind. The two liked each other. 'I'll give you your choice. I know you don't like grinding the grain with the mortar and pestle, but that needs doing. I could use some water from the cistern. And there's a large basket of uncarded wool that needs cleaning and spinning, then I can weave it.'

Nyresa made her choice quickly. 'I'll fetch some water, Thratta.'

The slave smiled. They both knew this was the easiest choice and provided the best chance for Nyresa to meet and chat with Glyka. 'Fix your hair a bit first, Nyresa. Your pretty headband needs tidying.' She smiled at the twelve-year-old with her long, curly black hair. 'It would look very nice tied with a flower in the front.'

Nyresa tossed her a cross look but began slowly combing through handfuls of wavy hair, finding an unpleasant number of little snarls. 'I should just wrap my hair in a band of cloth, the way you do, and hide it,' she scowled.

Thratta laughed. 'Don't you be rude about my sakkos.

22

I need it to keep my hair out of the food. Now, no more dark looks. Hurry to the cistern and home again. You do feel all right to go?' she asked casually while shooting a look at Nyresa.

Nyresa nodded, picked up the water jug, and headed east, towards the Agora. She thought about showing off her balancing skills by walking with the empty jug on her head, but instead held it close to her chest with both hands.

She headed straight for the cistern, a large hole, enclosed and partly covered by stone slabs. Fixed sideways across the top of the cistern was a pole with a rope and net attached. Slipping the jug into the net, she slowly lowered it by rope into the hole, allowing the gathered rainwater to enter its mouth and fill it entirely. Absorbed in the process, she hadn't noticed Glyka arrive. When Glyka's hands joined hers to haul up the jug, she turned in surprise and greeted her warmly. To look into her large, lustrous eyes and beautiful face, surrounded by honey-brown hair, comforted Nyresa almost as much as her grandmother's soothings.

But Glyka's eyes were not lustrous; they were red. She had been crying.

'What is it, Glyka? Are you all right?'

'Of course I am,' Glyka said. 'It's *you* I am worried about. The whole town is. Are *you* all right?'

Nyresa blushed deeply. How embarrassing! 'Yes, I'm fine. I just fainted. Oh, but Glyka,' she went on in a rush, 'do you know what my grandmother told me yesterday? She is taking me to Athens, to live with my cousin. My grandmother is going on a pilgrimage and, Glyka, we'll be gone for a long time!' She turned an agonized expression to her friend, knowing how upset she too would be.

To Nyresa's surprise, Glyka just stood in silence, looking at her. 'Nyresa, last night I too learned something. My parents have decided to move to Cyrene – before next summer.'

'Cyrene!' Nyresa exclaimed. Cyrene, on the north African coast . . . People drowned who set off to Cyrene.

Nyresa's look of fear brought an instant and practical rebuke from Glyka. 'Just because your father drowned sailing to Cyrene doesn't mean we will. Cyrene is Thira's colony; Thirans and Cyreneans sail back and forth across the Mediterranean all the time. Anyway, my parents knew about Epiktiti's pilgrimage and told me last night, so I've had time to think how we can stay in touch. Here is my plan. You take my favourite pigeon, Miron, to Athens. In time, when you are settled, send him back to me with your news. Some time after that I should go to Cyrene. But when you return to Thira, we can write to each other, using Thira's merchant ships as couriers.'

Nyresa smiled into Glyka's still-red eyes. She knew how much Glyka loved Miron. To be without him for months was a sacrifice she would make only for her closest friend. How confusing it was to have their lives change so quickly. Yesterday, to leave Thira for months or years seemed horrific; now Glyka's prospect of leaving forever lay before Nyresa. Nyresa thought she was the one forced out of the nest, but it turned out that Glyka too must move.

'Of course,' Glyka added wryly, 'things can change. The will of the gods is hard to follow.'

The two friends exchanged the same expression: a sad smile, made from pressed lips. Nyresa picked up her water jug and they walked off together to Thratta.

5. FESTIVAL

Over the next two weeks, before the festival to the gods, the girls met every day. Sometimes they talked about their futures, sometimes they did not. On the day of the festival, the priestess to Artemis and the priest to Apollo stood before the Temple of Apollo, their backs to the sea. Standing against the setting sun, the priestess and priest were outlined in black. All the inhabitants of the island stood before them, their faces shining, bathed in the last golden light of the day. Behind and on the right of the Thirans lay the cemetery, where their ancestors had been buried over the past seven hundred years. Behind them and to the left lay the Agora and their homes.

Apollo's priest spoke first. 'Every year we gather to thank Apollo for the fertility of our crops and animals. We thank Artemis for our healthy children. As our ancestors have taught us, we first worship the earth, as symbolized by the ram's horn of power, and the rams' horns hung with the grapes of fecundity. Tonight our youth dance to celebrate all that we worship: the earth, our health and,' he paused for effect, 'our island's future.'

Apollo's priest stepped back, Epiktiti stepped forwards.

She raised her arms, calling upon Artemis to receive the offering of Thira. She raised a shallow silver bowl, then, replacing it, raised a pottery drinking horn, showing the crowd its beautiful painted bull's head shape. She poured red wine from the horn into the shallow bowl and, holding the bowl in both hands, offered it to the sky, to Artemis. As she sang a prayer, she gently tipped the red wine on to the ground, pouring her libation to the goddess. The sound of her deep voice floated over the silent crowd and across the city, into the night. Now women from the crowd came forward with baskets of offerings for the goddess – of flowers, fruit, wreaths and branches. They laid their baskets around the altar and returned to their men and children.

Epiktiti spoke. 'In a few days, my granddaughter and I will depart for Attica.' The crowd shifted uneasily. 'My granddaughter will live in Athens with her father's family, while I undergo a pilgrimage.'

Epiktiti paused to gather in everyone's attention. 'I go to ask the gods what we are to do, how we are to act. I seek to know how our gods want us to face the Persian threat in future years. While I am away my fellow priests and priestesses will guide you.

'Each day, as I sit on my stone bench overlooking the sea, Poseidon, Apollo and Zeus come to me. They send their messengers, the sea, the sun and the eagles. We are surrounded by our gods, cradled in their powers. They will protect me, my granddaughter, and each one of you. Pray for us all while we are gone. I will return wiser in the ways of our gods and will use my wisdom to guide us. Trust in our gods, our fate is in their hands. Artemis, goddess of the moon and the hunt, and her brother, Apollo, the god of light and prophecy, the god of harmony, radiant with grace and beauty, will watch over the people of Thira. We need not fear. Praise be to Apollo and Artemis!'

Then drumbeats filled the air, flutes piped their breathy music into the dark, hand harps roused and moved the listening crowd. The people of Thira began to clap and rhythmically stamp their feet as a very young girl carrying a basket of grain and a knife passed through them towards the altar. The little girl walked up to Apollo's priest and stood quietly by his side. Then the seven maidens, girls aged ten, eleven and twelve, chosen by Epiktiti, entered in single file, hand in hand. Nyresa and Glyka were among them. Epiktiti lit a flame on the altar. Around the flame, the seven danced solemnly to the hard stamping and clapping of the people. The girls represented the future fertility of their people and, symbolically, of their crops. The people saw in the maidens all hope for survival. Nyresa looked across the circle at Glyka, whose eyes were fixed on her. Each girl knew the other was shy to be performing in front of everyone, but they knew their dance was important and serious.

Now came the sacrifice. A clean kill would prophesy the success of next year's crops. Everyone said a silent prayer to Apollo. Nyresa saw a group of men at the side of the temple step back: behind them stood a magnificent ox, huge, glossy black, with extraordinary horns and a tail thicker than a whip. Epiktiti went to the little girl with the basket, took up some grain and scattered it along the ground. Then Apollo's priest approached the little girl and removed the knife from her basket. With all the citizens watching he turned to the gigantic ox, stared straight into the animal's eyes and, in a swift double motion, took hold of one horn, slightly raising and twisting the animal's head. Nyresa watched intently as he sliced clear through the arteries at the neck, causing a river of blood to pour out on to the loose grains on the ground. The ox looked up at the priest, then dropped dead to the ground.

The crowd roared their relief. They cheered and clapped. Nyresa was relieved. An auspicious kill. The city would live another year. Apollo and Artemis would protect them. Their crops would be good, and the future was promising.

As the cheering pounded through Nyresa, seven teenage boys in ideal physical condition, earnest and eager, stepped forth from the crowd. They ran past the temple of Apollo, and along the path to the very western tip of the mountain, stopping at the hard-pressed ground, the platform where only two weeks ago Nyresa had sat, dangling her swinging legs over the cliff edge. As the boys assembled, the men of Thira pulled the ox away from the front of the temple and the priest butchered it, skilfully cutting out the choicest pieces to offer to Apollo, hacking up the rest in chunks to be cooked and distributed to every citizen.

The athletes formed themselves into a circle. They danced in perfect harmony, moving faster and faster in time to the rhythmic clapping of the people. Their beauty and strength mirrored the ox's beauty and strength, and complemented the dancing of the girls. All the Thirans felt themselves blessed to be living on Thira. They had no thought of Persians. Tonight they celebrated: there was no drought, the citizens and their children were healthy, the harvest good. These were good omens for the future.

After the festival, tired dancers and proud parents walked home under the stars. Everyone had eaten well. Tomorrow they would face the future with renewed hope. Some Thirans walked up to their homes on the northern plateau, some to theirs in the south. Nyresa, separated in the events from her grandmother, walked alone until she felt a hand slip into hers. It was Glyka's.

The two walked together in silence. Tonight they had danced before all of Thira. As twelve-year-old girls, they knew their childhoods were about to come to an abrupt end. Their dance was called the partheneion, which means 'dance of the virgins'. It meant that they would soon be ready to marry. Marriage followed childhood so quickly that brides ritually brought their toys to Artemis's temple the night before their wedding. Neither Nyresa nor Glyka had thought about marriage and had hardly ever spoken to boys, but they accepted, especially after tonight's dance, that their lives would soon change. In the dark silence of this night, as they walked, each thought how her life already had changed.

In a small voice Nyresa said, 'Glyka, I don't want to leave Thira and my mother's grave and my kore and you.'

Glyka was silent for a few steps. Dropping Nyresa's hand, she turned to face her. 'Nyresa, we have no choice – you will go to Athens and I to Cyrene. Your mother's grave and your kore will be waiting for your return. As for our seeing each other again, we may well.'

'You know we won't,' Nyresa cried.

'I don't know. I'll tell you something very private that I believe. I believe we will make new friends who remind us of each other and that through these friends we will remain close. I will find a good friend in Cyrene and I will tell her my most secret thoughts. And you will find a girl in Athens who reminds you of me and she will steady and comfort you. Even if we don't meet again, one of us may meet the other's child, or our children may come to know each other. Somehow, the gods will help us find each other.'

With that Glyka turned, looked back to wave goodbye, and walked down the street towards her house. Nyresa watched her go. The full moon, Artemis's sign, shone white light on to the mountaintop. The eerie glow transformed Thira's stone houses and cobbled streets into a ghostly city.

Nyresa was thinking. She had lost her mother, then her father, and now Glyka. In two days she would leave her island and, soon after, lose her grandmother. She faced the black sea for a moment, then turned quickly towards her house.

II

Persephone fainted in terror. She awoke lying on a huge bed in a huge room. No one else was there. Slowly she crept out of the room and through dark corridors until she saw a door opening on to palace gardens and orchards. There the gloom was less intense. She dashed across the gardens to a small, hidden door but found it locked. She ran around to the palace entry gates and found that they too were locked. Nothing moved or sounded. She turned to the orchard. Perhaps there she could escape. Then she heard the heavy tread of boots behind her.

Demeter's heart was broken. For nine days and nights she scoured the earth in search of her daughter. Then, on the tenth day, she spoke with two shepherds who had seen the chariot and the black horses and had heard the terrible thud of the hooves and the girl's frightened cries. What they had not seen was the charioteer's face.

She approached Helios, the sun god, he who sees all, and forced him to disclose the abductor's identity. It was Hades who had taken Persephone. Demeter knew he never would have done so without Zeus's approval. She plotted her revenge.

Earth felt the scourge. Plants ceased to grow, fruits to flower, grains to rise. Trees could not bear fruit. There was nothing to eat. No *infants were born to any living creature. Demeter swore an oath: earth would remain barren until her daughter was returned to her. The human race — Zeus's plaything — was in danger of extinction.*

JOY

492 BC, LATE SUMMER

1. PASSAGE

Two days after the festival, Nyresa and Epiktiti stood on a narrow stretch of sand at the edge of the caldera. They were ready to board their ship. As anchoring was impossible in the limitlessly deep basin, the ship was tied with a great length of rope to a boulder projecting from the slope. To distract herself, Nyresa counted the layers of coloured rock in the surrounding slopes. She counted forty-three. Each colour was created by a fresh explosion of the volcano, all having occurred after the mighty eruption that blew the mountain into the sky.

Still looking up, Nyresa caught sight of Glyka making her way by donkey, following the zigzag dirt path from the top of the slope to the bottom. Nyresa grinned. She could see Miron's cage, attached somehow to Glyka's waist, bouncing against her leg.

Soon the girls were saying goodbye, embracing, promising to see each other again. The city of Thira had already bidden them goodbye and good luck, hours ago. But Glyka wanted to come and say her last farewell here, in the caldera.

'Nyresa, I know you will take good care of Miron. Here is a bag of his favourite seeds. They're easy to get. Anyway, this amount should last over a month. He doesn't eat very much each day.'

Nyresa took the looped handle of a wicker cage from Glyka. Inside, a tiny pale-grey homing pigeon was making whirring and cackling noises, jerking its beady eyes up and down, trying to see everything.

'But I have a final surprise for you,' Glyka said. She untied a second parcel from her waist and gave it to Nyresa, whose eyes were round with curiosity and delight.

'Honey pastry! Oh, thank you, Glyka. Please thank your mother.' Nyresa was delighted. Greedily she looked into the bag and saw a huge slice of the very sweet, layered pastry with honey and crushed nuts in between. As Nyresa, smiled into Glyka's eyes, tears fell down her cheeks. From now on she would associate the sweetness of honey with the sadness of parting.

Nyresa and Epiktiti were rowed to the ship, boarded, and the sails were hoisted. Nyresa waved goodbye to Glyka, who was loyally waiting on the stretch of sand until the ship was out of sight. As the ship slid out of the caldera, Nyresa looked one last time at the basin with its steep slopes, at the treeless clifftops, and at the blue, blue water. She remembered the yellow, gaseous bubbles and the silver flashes of fish below the surface. Rock and water, she thought, that is my home. But my home is also my mother's grave, my kore, and my view from the mountaintop. Goodbye all, she whispered to herself. Goodbye Thratta, Glyka.

Epiktiti stood beside her on the deck, looking at Thira. 'Apollo and Artemis will watch over our home, Nyresa. The gods made us and they will protect us.'

Twelve days of sailing passed. Nyresa began to lose all hope of ever arriving. Then, out of nowhere, land appeared – Attica! Their ship hugged the land and for hours sailed parallel to rounded, undulating mountain ranges. The mountains were low now, with only a narrow beach separating them from the sea, the Saronic Gulf. Nyresa was pleased to see that, unlike on volcanic Thira, there were forests on the hills and trees alongside the water. But mostly her impression was of rocky land and sandy soil. She missed Thira's marble mountains; these mountains were tame in comparison.

Then they reached their port: Phaleron. From here they would make their way to Athens by land. Nyresa leapt up to the rail to see. Sailors surrounded her as they prepared the ship to dock. She overheard two speaking.

'Did you hear what that tall passenger – the one who got on last stop – said? About Mardonius?' said the first.

'I did. And I heard more from others. Not good,' said the second, shaking his head.

'No,' the first returned. 'So his fleet has met up with the Persian army and together they're moving west. Those Persians are coming to Athens, mark my words.'

The second nodded. 'And slaughtering peoples who never raised a hand to them along the way – Thracians, Macedonians . . .'

'Macedonians? They're *that* close to Athens? What's the government doing about it?'

'Nothing. Every citizen of Athens has a vote, and what sort of government do we get?'

'They spend all their time arguing, and what do they do? Nothing.'

'Come on, you two,' a voice of authority called out. 'Keep gabbing like that and we'll still be sitting here when Mardonius arrives! Get a move on!'

Nyresa's eyes widened.

'So how much longer do they say we have until the Persians arrive?' the first man asked, as they began grabbing ropes and untying knots.

The second gave a short laugh. 'They'll be here before the fish your wife bought this morning starts to stink!'

When Nyresa hurried to tell her grandmother what she had heard, she found her deep in conversation with the captain of the ship. Nyresa saw her touch her lips, forehead and heart, and knew that she had heard about Mardonius. Yet when Nyresa began to move towards her, eager to question her, she stopped in surprise: Epiktiti had turned to face the sun-drenched plain and, far from looking fearful, she was rapt in wonder. Nyresa stared at her, then towards the plain. There, just to the right of centre, was a massive rocky plateau surmounted by a shining marble temple. Leading directly to this plateau, straight up from Phaleron, was a dusty-white road. And surrounding the gigantic rock was a swarm of the greatest number of houses Nyresa had ever seen – or ever imagined.

'What is that?' she whispered, breathlessly.

Epiktiti smiled. 'Athens.'

Already things were happening too quickly for Nyresa to respond. She stood in amazement, forgetting Mardonius.

'Do you know why you were named Nyresa?' Epiktiti quietly asked her. 'It means "near the Acropolis". During your mother's pregnancy, when you were still in her belly, she had a recurring dream of the Acropolis. She kept saying you were linked to it in some way. That is why she gave you your name.'

Nyresa sneaked a look at Epiktiti. She was mesmerized by the mixture of pride and dignity emanating from her grandmother. On Thira, Epiktiti was commanding and respected, but she was also a familiar figure, the midwife at every birth, the officiating priestess at every ceremony to Artemis. Now she seemed more remote, somehow more serious.

Soon Nyresa was whisked into a cart that was hitched to mules, while Epiktiti shouted bossy orders at everyone. Nyresa loved looking around at all the buildings. The cart began moving and her eyes darted here, there, everywhere. I'm acting like Miron, she smiled to herself.

The cart soon left Phaleron and started up the straight, dusty road to Athens. Directly before them the city itself loomed and Nyresa was astonished.

2. FIRST SIGHT

They entered the city from its southern, seaward side. Nyresa sat in the front seat of the cart, beside the driver, with Epiktiti behind her, and said nothing, just looked. As the cart passed through the gate in the old circuit wall surrounding the city, what she saw was beyond her wildest imaginings. Houses, houses, houses – as far as the eye could see. Some stood on their own, some in rows, some in blocks of what looked like multiple dwellings. Their walls were yellowish, often with contrasting earthen browns, blues, greens, reds and whites. They had been plastered smooth and had narrow slit windows cut into their sides. Wavy terracotta tiles covered the roofs. The more prosperous houses had elaborate wooden doors, with patterns made with iron bolts and knobs, some even with moulded lions' heads or miniature shields.

Thira, a city of two hundred people, only had stone houses. Here before Nyresa stretched thousands of earthen-brick houses and thousands of people.

The roads were jammed. Their cart could hardly make forward progress through all the people, carts, horses. Everywhere Nyresa looked, she saw different styles, different appearances. Women whose faces and shoulders were covered by cloaks or shawls called himations; women with uncovered faces, laughing and talking, shouting and scolding, and men of all ages, all appearances, sometimes in clothes that suggested their foreignness, sometimes in

38

the Greek chiton with the himation cloak. Slaves too. The male ones in their exomis, a tunic belted at the waist, with one shoulder bare. The female slaves less easy to spot, often hard to distinguish from poorer foreign women. Everyone was moving, buying, selling, transporting, unloading.

Nyresa had never seen such a volume of activity or heard such noise. After a while she turned to Epiktiti and said, 'Grandmother, why do some women wrap their shawls around their heads, covering most of their faces? They must be so hot – and they can hardly see!'

'Do you notice anything else about them?' Epiktiti asked.

Nyresa looked intently into the crowd as their cart rumbled along. 'Well, there aren't many of them. And they walk with their heads down, and always seem to be accompanied by a servant.'

'That's because they are Athenian ladies, Nyresa. They are upper class and follow very strict rules of behaviour. They rarely go out and, if they do, they cover their faces.'

'Must we cover our faces?' Nyresa asked worriedly.

'No, my dear. We are not Athenians. To them we are foreigners. Foreign women do not have to cover their faces.'

Nyresa turned with amazement to her grandmother. 'But you are a head priestess to Artemis! Doesn't that make you upper class, even if you are from Thira?'

Epiktiti smiled. 'I will be respected and allowed to enter and worship on the Acropolis because I am a priestess to Artemis but, as I am not an Athenian upper-class lady, I am not required to cover my face when out in public.'

Nyresa still looked worried. 'So I don't have to cover my face . . . but am I allowed on the Acropolis?'

'No. Only when you are accompanied by a priest or priestess or an Athenian citizen can you enter the Acropolis.' She watched her granddaughter closely, seeing how she would respond to this new limitation to her freedom. But Nyresa, busy observing, kept her reactions to herself.

They entered the Agora. Here was wonder indeed, a vast open space filled with jostling crowds and circled with imposing buildings. But when Nyresa looked up and saw the Acropolis with the temple of Athena overlooking all, she was astonished. The temple was wonderful!

Epiktiti ordered the driver to turn west, down a narrow street jammed with houses but free of traffic. As the cart rolled along the packed-earth street, Nyresa gazed with admiration into doors and courtyards holding arguing families or lazy cats. Now and again people looked up with curiosity at the girl and her cart, but mostly they stepped back nonchalantly, barely a cubit or so, to let the cart pass.

At last Epiktiti ordered the cart to stop before a stout wooden door set into a long, smooth-plastered wall. Nyresa watched with growing trepidation. The driver knocked on the door, gave his message to the formidable old female slave who answered and stepped aside, while out rushed a man – no doubt the uncle – and a woman, his wife. They greeted Epiktiti and then Nyresa with great noise and energy.

Epiktiti, Nyresa and the slave Thratta had long lived in an all-female household – Nyresa was not expecting the force of her uncle's personality. A handsome, short, energetic man, he rushed over to the cart and helped Epiktiti down before she was quite ready. Clearly delighted with this arrival of his brother's family, he spun about, bursting with a host's pride. He then helped Nyresa down, while simultaneously urging his wife to busy herself unloading the baggage. His wife, though equally welcoming, seemed somewhat hesitant. She allowed the old woman slave, whom she called Tunnis, to order her back to the house and let the others get on with the unloading. Nyresa thought this was peculiar and very different from her grandmother and Thratta. In the confusion, Epiktiti managed to pay the driver who, casting resentful looks at Tunnis, left as soon as possible. Nyresa stood a bit to the side, uncomfortable and aware her cousin had not come out.

Her uncle shooed the three women inside the courtyard as though herding chickens. Nyresa smiled to herself at her grandmother's surprise. She was not used to men telling her what to do.

Once inside the courtyard, Nyresa suddenly felt shy. She signalled to her grandmother that she wanted a quick, private word. 'Grandmother, you aren't leaving right away, are you, not tomorrow?'

Epiktiti held Nyresa's eyes. 'I will not leave Athens while there is a threat. Now, you need to feel settled. I'll ask your aunt where your room is – or I'll ask Tunnis,' she added under her breath, already aware of the power structure in this new household.

Tunnis, hovering and efficient, had gathered Nyresa's

bags and started up the wooden staircase that led from the courtyard to the first-floor balcony and bedrooms. Tunnis was quite old, perhaps sixty, a big woman and powerfully built. She wore her grey hair in one long plait coiled into an imposing crown. She had a very intelligent face but small, suspicious eyes and a little, pursed mouth. It would not be good to disobey her was Nyresa's first thought, as she dutifully followed. Her uncle called up to her another jolly welcome with many promises of happy times to come, while her aunt, still vaguely baffled by these newcomers, smiled encouragingly. Nyresa was aware of other servants bustling about the house but saw no sign of her cousin.

Once in her simple room Nyresa sat on her bed, gently placing Miron's wicker cage beside it, and collapsed, asleep before she knew it. Tunnis must have stayed to unpack her things but Nyresa never heard her. All night she dreamed of the Agora in Thira, of murmurings and urgent whisperings in the city's meeting place. The murmurings persisted throughout her dreams, though she could never make them out.

3. RHODE

When she awoke the next morning, she saw with pleasure the freshly painted red walls of her bedroom, the delicate wooden chair with its webbed seat, and the black-glazed jug in the corner. Miron was cooing contentedly and Nyresa could tell that someone – Tunnis – had changed his water and given him just the sort of seed he loved. How did she know? Nyresa wondered. Quietly she slipped out of bed and began to explore.

There was an open patio just outside her bedroom, on the street side. Then she saw a massive cage full of homing pigeons. She burst out laughing. This was the murmuring she had heard all night in her dreams! At least fifteen pigeons eyed her suspiciously, fluffing out their necks and ruffling their wings. They all made Miron-like noises. Immediately she got Miron but, suddenly unsure, placed his cage beside the huge cage.

'Oh, he can go in with the others,' a girl's gentle voice said. 'They like to be together.'

Whirling around, Nyresa saw a tall, slender girl leaning against the doorframe. Something about the way she stood made Nyresa feel the girl needed to sit.

'Good morning,' Nyresa politely said, standing. 'I am Nyresa and —'

'I am Rhode,' she interrupted, smiling. 'We are cousins,' she added. 'I'm sorry I didn't greet you yesterday. It was one of my bad days.'

Nyresa, though ready to dislike Rhode, or at least resent her for inspiring Epiktiti's plan for her to live in Athens, melted. There was only gentle sweetness in her bearing, manner and words. 'Would you like a chair?' Nyresa asked her.

'Oh,' Rhode half laughed, 'yes, I suppose I would.' She glanced quickly at Nyresa with a rueful look. Nyresa was too embarrassed to ask what her illness was, but quickly got the webbed chair from her bedroom. As Rhode sat she said, plainly and directly, 'I'm not strong. The doctors tell me I have a disease. My legs used to be fine but now work less and less well. Some days are better than others, if I rest a lot, but I fear I have a wasting condition and one day will not be able to walk.'

Not knowing what to say, Nyresa cast an alarmed look at Rhode.

'Don't worry,' Rhode said. 'I've grown used to it and it isn't catching. I just,' and here she extended her arms and gently flapped them up and down, 'move slowly from one room to the next, like some insect with long, long legs.' Both girls laughed and the ice was broken.

'Is this your pigeon, then?' Rhode asked Nyresa, smiling. 'What is his – or is it a her – name?'

'Miron,' Nyresa answered, sharing the smile. 'He belongs to my best friend on Thira, Glyka. I'm to send him back home to her with a message when I feel settled.'

'What a kind thing to do,' Rhode exclaimed. 'I like birds, too – as you can see. Some of these belong to me but some belong to my friend, Agariste. We send messages all the time to each other.'

'Do you? Why not meet instead?' Nyresa asked.

'Oh, Agariste is an Athenian lady and is meant to stay at home, with her little son. She visits relatives and the ill, and attends funerals, but mostly she keeps to her home. Once in a great while she can visit me but, thanks to the pigeons, we talk every day. We first met at Demeter's temple, called the Eleusinium, when I was eight and she was fourteen. I was hardly lame then. She was helping to teach the little girls the dance, the partheneion. Since then she has married and had a son.'

While Rhode was talking, Nyresa looked at her carefully. I know what she looks like, Nyresa thought, with a little burst of delight. She looks like those water birds I've seen painted on large storage jugs. The one we had at home to hold fish sauce was painted with reeds, a dragonfly, an osier, crocuses and myrtle, and a long, tall, lovely bird – like Rhode. Nyresa's face fell slightly as she remembered the bird's graceful bearing, one leg crooked, as it bent down to drink. For Rhode, as she leaned against the door jamb, it had not been so easy.

'What were you thinking?' Rhode inquired with, Nyresa blushed to realize, an unnerving intelligence in her eyes.

Abashed, Nyresa lied. 'About the Persians. Yesterday the sailor who helped tie up our ship at Phaleron said Mardonius, with his fleet and army, were headed for Athens.'

'Yes,' Rhode said. 'They are coming, conquering, extending Darius's power as they make their way towards us. Yesterday I heard they are headed next for a city called Eretria, on an island across from Attica. They should get there in, perhaps, a week or less. Then they will be only a few days away from Athens.'

The two girls looked at each other in silence. Nyresa was sorry she'd raised the subject and sought to change it. She looked at Rhode's thick, black hair, woven in one long braid with a little net holding the ends in a round knot or bun, and realized she wore it as a parthenos – a style proclaiming a maiden's readiness to marry.

'Rhode, you are a parthenos! Are you going to be married?' As soon as she spoke she felt misgivings.

Again that intelligence flashed through Rhode's face. There was a wryness, a sophistication there that made Nyresa feel very young. 'My dear cousin, yes, I am a parthenos and fifteen years of age, but I will never marry because of my lameness. At least that's what my mother keeps telling me. And when the Persians come I shall probably be killed for it too. No one wants a lame wife – and a lame slave is useless.' She looked into the distance, dry amusement in her face. 'Perhaps if Mardonius orders his men to carry me, I just might be taken to Susa to be one of Darius's wives.'

Nyresa was shocked and didn't know how to respond. I will be like Glyka, she thought, sweet but practical and clear. Taking a deep breath, she said, 'Do not tease me. Instead, tell me more about Agariste.'

Her raised face seemed to Nyresa full of thoughts and understanding. 'She is my good friend. She is twenty-one and the wife of Xanthippus, a commander in the army on duty in Magna Graecia. They have one little boy, aged five. Her husband is rarely in Athens, but he is very strict and has given orders that she not go out of the house much. If I were an Athenian lady, though, my lameness would be an acceptable excuse for Agariste to visit me often.'

'You're not an Athenian lady?' Nyresa prodded, feeling awkward but curious.

Rhode laughed. 'No. Although I was born in Athens, I was born to a metic and his wife.' She held up a finger when she saw Nyresa draw breath to ask what a metic was. 'A metic is an inhabitant of Athens who is not a citizen. Most metics are craftsmen and artists who have come to Athens to seek their fortune. But my father – your uncle – who came from Thira, is quite a well-off merchant. Since the reforms of twenty years ago, metics are now allowed to vote, so they are almost citizens. Thanks to my father's wealth and the democratic reforms, Xanthippus has decided I am an acceptable friend for his wife, but prefers her to keep it private.' Her eyes sparkled as she gazed directly into Nyresa's nervous little face. 'It works very well for us both. Agariste is kind and clever and we've been friends for seven years.'

There were too many new considerations here. Nyresa gave a grimace of a smile, trying to carry on her part of the conversation. 'Perhaps one day I could meet her, if ...' Nyresa stopped, embarrassed to remember Rhode wasn't upper class enough to merit visits. She changed topic. 'Perhaps, can we go out?' She gave a little exasperated cry. 'Oh, Rhode, I can't say anything right. Can you go out? I mean, can you walk?'

Rhode laughed. 'Don't worry. We'll get all these questions behind us and they won't come up again. I can go out, on a chair carried by slaves – a fine arrangement but expensive, so I don't do it often. You certainly can go out whenever you wish. After all, we are foreign, not Athenian ladies; we can go out with uncovered faces anywhere, any time.' Rhode turned a poised but open face to Nyresa. 'Oh, Nyresa, I have dreamed about your living here and going out into Athens every day, having adventures, shopping at the Agora, climbing the Acropolis, even visiting the Pynx and the Areopagus – and coming back to tell me everything!'

'Going where?' Nyresa laughed, relieved by this more familiar tone. 'I don't even know *what* let alone *where* such places are. I think we passed through the Agora yesterday, and I know I saw the Acropolis with the temple to Athena. Rhode, I've never seen so many people and houses in my life. From Phaleron to Athens to this house I was terrified.'

Rhode realized she was serious. 'Well, I've made a plan for today which will help you get used to our city. Tunnis is to take you on a tour of the Agora, so you can start helping with our shopping.'

Nyresa's face darkened. 'Shopping? That's what Thratta does for us on Thira.'

'Is Thratta your slave?' Rhode asked. Nyresa nodded. 'Ah, but you don't know Athens. The Agora is the best of places. It is where everyone sees everyone else, where all the news and gossip is exchanged. And the fish queue is the most important place of all. There you'll see the city's most powerful men, and the most shocking of its elegant hostesses.' She grinned. 'You'll get all the best scandal.'

Nyresa's eyes widened as she looked at Rhode. Elegant hostesses! It sounded fun.

Rhode continued, 'Tomorrow Epiktiti has arranged to take us to the Acropolis to give thanks to Athena and Artemis and pray for the gods' protection of Thira and of

Athens. I'm worried that the news of Mardonius and the Persians might affect our plans.'

Nyresa liked the way Rhode spoke. 'Affect our plans' meant 'Athens may be burned to the ground any day now, me dead, and you taken into slavery'. Yes, she liked Rhode's manner. She realized too that her presence would probably make a big difference in Rhode's life. For herself, she wanted to be back home on Thira, with Glyka and Thratta and her grandmother. Yet she couldn't ask for a more poised and interesting cousin.

'I don't think our plans will be affected,' Nyresa replied, enjoying this new game of understatement. 'My grandmother has faith in the gods' protection.'

'Fine,' Rhode smiled. 'Good.'

4. AGORA

Tunnis was formidable. She was opinionated, bossy and physically intimidating. That she was an old woman made her more frightening. Nyresa was alarmed at the prospect of going out alone with her. She resolved to be brave – brave as Glyka. So she chose her red tunic for its boldness and adventure. She vowed not just to face this excursion but also to reach out for it. She and Tunnis left the house immediately after Nyresa and Rhode's conversation, to get to the stalls early.

Tunnis strode ahead, leaving Nyresa to keep up. I must remember this route, she thought. I can't get lost tomorrow. When the late-afternoon sun shone on the temple yesterday, making it gleam, I knew I was facing north, with the sun setting to my left. And when our cart turned into this street, I remember thinking we now were headed north. So now we must be going south. The Agora is directly south or maybe south-west of Rhode's house. Then she made a tisking sound, irritated with herself. All I have to do to get to the Agora is to keep the Acropolis on my left and when I return home keep it on my right. Stupid me.

As she hurried behind Tunnis, Nyresa tried to count street corners but she soon gave up. There were too many. Athens was nothing like Thira, which had only two main streets. On Thira, all the stone houses lined up against these two streets, sometimes one behind the other but always at right angles to the street itself. Here everything was different. Instead of stone, the houses were made of clay (later she would learn, mixed with limestone) and wood and tile; the streets were made of packed earth; and there were trees. Nyresa loved these trees that were scattered about the city in clusters, swaying in a strong wind and giving wonderful relief from the hot sun. Nyresa did not yet know any of their names. For her, a child of volcanic Thira, trees were simply marvels.

When the street they were on opened directly into the Agora, Tunnis bustled straight into the jammed open space. Nyresa, dropping all pretence of dignity, grabbed on to a fold of the old woman's linen tunic and hung on. They plunged into the crowds. As Tunnis pushed forwards, Nyresa in tow, they passed many tables under colourful awnings, selling all manner of food, drink, objects and artefacts. One table they passed sold nuts of many kinds: almonds, hazelnuts, pine nuts, nuts from Persia and Egypt. Nearby stood a table displaying olives, Egyptian beans, dates and other dried fruits for sale. There were tables laden with jewellery, gold earrings, bone and bronze hairpins, portrait rings, gold bracelets, carved gems. In an open booth, Nyresa saw men having their hair cut by a barber; nearby she saw a table packed with beautiful perfume bottles; further off, a row of tables laden with pottery in an array of shapes.

Trying to get her bearings in this sea of people and stalls, Nyresa looked all around her and then up. She gasped. There, right above them, was Athena's temple on top of the Acropolis. Of course she knew she was near the Acropolis as she and Tunnis had walked around its base to get to the Agora. But from the ground the rock face of the citadel was just a continuous stone slope, blocking all view and light. Suddenly now, from this distance, she could see the top. Her stomach rolled over: how she wanted to go up, to be up there, to see the view, to feel the wind . . .

Oh, to be back in Thira on her mountaintop! The temple drew her with its beauty but it was the hilltop that called to her, commanded her. All her life she had associated safety with height. Now here she was, low on the ground and not even allowed to climb the citadel. Praying to Glyka, then to Artemis, then to her grandmother, she willed herself to grow calm.

Tunnis had not noticed her yearning or upset. Finally she stopped before a table piled with baskets of figs. 'How many owls for a shield's worth?' she asked. Nyresa stared at her.

'Two talents, my beauty,' the crusty seller replied.

'I am not your beauty and mind your manners,' Tunnis snapped. 'Here is one talent. And wrap them up well, mind you.' She slapped a coin and a narrow strip of wool on the table and turned away. With a sour look, the old seller placed a lead weight on one arm of his scales then gently placed fig after fig into the bowl on the scale's other arm. When the two arms balanced, he removed the figs and wrapped them in Tunnis's strip of wool.

Meanwhile, swinging cheerfully down the wooded hill just west of the Agora came a young man, aged about seventeen. He was headed to the Agora for food. He was hungry. He had worked all day at the blacksmith's shop where he lodged. The wooded hill, called Kolonos Agoratos, was situated roughly between the Acropolis and the Agora; it was the centre of all metalworking and blacksmithing in Athens. The youth had had a hard morning chopping wood for the forge, but an easier afternoon returning shod horses to their masters and collecting others to be shod. He loved working with horses and was very good with them. Now all he could think about was *food*.

Being young, it was appropriate he should be wearing the short tunic called a chiton, but as he was well built and fit, wearing it was a secret conceit for him. He was tall, with tightly curled black hair, handsome, with symmetrical features, a wide brow and full lips. He knew how good he looked. Now, however, he was searching for money in the folds that served as pockets in his chiton. He only found half an obol. Six obols was a day's work. One obol could buy him a big jug of wine. If only he had a handful of drachmas! Visions of slabs of lamb, available only at religious festivals, floated through his mind. Fish he dismissed as too expensive, even anchovies and sprats. He could get a honey sweet, but just a small one that he'd down in a second. Oh, *food*! All right, he resigned himself, it'll have to be a hardboiled egg ... unless I can do a few tricks. He smiled to himself.

He came soon to the sale tables and began gliding expertly through the crowd. He liked this 'skimming'. Amid the crones dragged down by old age and shopping bags, he spun and dived like a seabird, looking at everything, happily aware that they took no notice of him. When he arrived at the table selling cooked eggs he played the part of the charming and hungry youth, while the crones around the table – server and served – were no less true to type, as disapproving and impatient old women. In fact, wild horses would not have been able to stop the old mothers from feeding him, he was so handsome and full of life; they just had to make him work for it. So he smiled and rubbed his hard belly and looked beseechingly into their faces, and they scowled and called for him to move away from the table, poking their old fingers into his muscular shoulder and waving him away with wrinkled hands. Soon he left the table with his arms full of food: two cooked eggs, a honey pastry, a little parcel of olives and a small jug of wine.

53

Delighted, he withdrew under a plane tree and began to wolf down the food, wiping his hands on his chiton while his cheeks were still stuffed and his jaws crunching. Then he saw Nyresa.

It may have been her scarlet tunic that drew his eye. She stood out among all the people and stalls and wares of the Agora. Her black curls, framing elegant, fine features, held his gaze. Then he saw the monster that was her chaperone – Tunnis – and kept his distance.

Nyresa, mesmerized by Tunnis and disorientated by the whole scene, did not notice the youth sitting nearby watching, amused. He was enjoying Tunnis's sharp tongue and the discomfort it gave the grizzled seller. As Tunnis and Nyresa moved on to an olive oil stall, the handsome boy followed lazily at a distance.

'I want four kotyles of oil and I'd better be able to see the goddess's head,' Tunnis declared. Nyresa had no idea what she was talking about but the serving woman clearly did. She held up a small jug with a squiggle of paint on the side. Tunnis nodded curtly and presented the woman with a large jug into which she carefully poured four measures of oil.

Tunnis now dragged Nyresa across the Agora to a very odd monument, where they stopped. It was a marble platform topped by ten male statues. A stone fence, chest high, surrounded the platform. The statues themselves were larger than life-size. Below their feet were noticeboards of some sort, one below each statue.

'This will orientate you in the Agora,' Tunnis declared.

'It is the monument of the Eponymous Heroes. The citizens of Athens are divided into ten tribes and each tribe's hero is sculpted here. See, there are ten statues.' She paused for a moment. Nyresa nodded. 'The notices beneath contain official proclamations, drafts of new laws, information about lawsuits and juries. If you need to get your bearings, just look for this monument. Here, let me show you.' As Tunnis took a step back from the fence, she bumped into someone. It was the lad from the fig stall and she gave him a scolding look. 'Our street is directly across the Agora, there.' She pointed due west, then started to move on again. The boy had disappeared.

Nyresa suddenly felt bewildered and exhausted. 'I'm sure I shall one day understand, Tunnis, but it is all so crowded and confusing. When can we go home?'

Tunnis was brusque and tough but she was not cruel. Her face softened as she took in this girl, now resembling a miserable, lost puppy. 'Don't cry now, young miss. We shall be home soon enough. As for what is confusing, it is easily explained. Coins in Athens have a picture of Athena on one side and of her owl on the other, so we call them "owls". Clear? "Laurium owls", because their silver is mined in Mount Laurium, in southern Attica. When you buy things, you want to be sure the seller isn't cheating you by selling you less in weight than you ordered. A standard weight is called a stater, nicknamed a knucklebone. A quarter stater is called a shield, and a sixth of a stater is called a turtle. Watch the seller's hands carefully as he places the weights on his scales. Each weight has on its top a bone, a turtle or a shield. Do you see? For olive oil or wine, the city provides special jugs with pictures of Athena or her owl on the side. Just make sure the seller uses one of those special jugs.'

Nyresa looked like she was either going to hit Tunnis or be sick. 'I don't feel well,' she mumbled.

'Nonsense, miss. But we shall rest. I'll take you to the quietest, most pleasant spot in the Agora. We can sit there and catch our breath.' And she bustled off again, though this time taking Nyresa's hand and casting solicitous glances at her as they sailed through the crowd. At a carefully maintained distance, the boy followed in their wake.

They walked west, to the altar of the Twelve Gods, a square, paved enclosure surrounded by a waist-high stone wall. In its centre was a simple stone altar but around its sides were lovely stone carvings of the twelve Olympian gods. Nyresa slid gratefully down the side of the wall, coming to rest on the stone paving. 'Anyone who needs refuge or help in any way is welcome here,' Tunnis told her quietly. She reached into her himation and drew out a little phial and gave it to Nyresa. It was water and wine, cool and sweet, the best Nyresa had ever tasted.

'Thank you,' she said, with just a hint of sarcasm. She had begun to hate this outing.

'Perhaps the Agora is a bit overwhelming,' Tunnis apologized. 'But I wanted you to learn its ways and not get cheated at the stalls. Some other day I shall show you the fountain house and the well where we get fresh water and the Tholos and the Bouleuterion where the government is.' She saw Nyresa's alarm and at last realized enough was enough. 'We shall go home,' she said. As she began to help Nyresa to her feet, she realized someone else was at her side. It was the same boy again. 'Do you mind?' she demanded imperiously, shaking him off while propelling Nyresa forwards. The boy held up both hands as though in surrender and, smiling, stepped back. Tunnis gave him a hard look, committing his features to memory and throwing him an absolutely clear warning to keep away. She shook her head in irritation.

Tunnis didn't see the boy then go sit on the ground next to a very pretty girl also at the altar of the Twelve Gods.

'What were you doing, you ridiculous boy?' the girl asked archly. 'Before I came in here to rest, I saw you trailing behind that crone and her curly-haired charge.' She pulled back in a mock-examination of the boy. 'I've known you for a year now, Cherson, and never seen you take an interest in any girls. Yet this one has caught your attention?' She must have been about his age, if not a year or two younger, but had a grown-up air that clearly made her his superior.

Cherson tried to deflect her accurate observations. 'You know I only care for you, Klio! The prettiest flute player in Athens. How could you think I could look at another?'

Klio sat, arms folded, and watched Nyresa and Tunnis as they walked through the Agora. 'So the great Cherson has finally been smitten. You know perfectly well I am engaged to a taverna keeper on the lovely island of Aegina.' Her whole mood suddenly deflated. 'Though I'll probably never see him again.'

Cherson put his arm around her shoulders and gave a little squeeze. 'We don't know what will happen,' he reassured her.

'No, we don't,' she agreed, and they sat in companionable silence in the midday sun.

5. ACROPOLIS

That evening the family dined lightly on platters of figs, eggs and olives. Nyresa and Rhode had their supper on the patio by the pigeon cage and were very happy. Over dinner, the adults spoke more about Mardonius's invasion. Kleomenes, Rhode's father, pointed out that so far there had been no general exodus to the mountains and that, personally, he and his wife had decided not to flee. Fleeing would bring them no more safety than staying in Athens. If Athens fell, so would all of mainland Greece and the islands. Epiktiti confided in them her powerful sense that Athens would not fall. Silently, she resolved to begin her pilgrimage the moment she determined that Athens was, at least temporarily, safe. Though encouraged by her certainty, Kleomenes sighed. All three agreed that it would be good for Epiktiti and the girls to pray tomorrow on the Acropolis.

Epiktiti retired to bed that evening worried. She lay in the dark imagining Mardonius's fleet, now in the middle of the Thracian Sea. Suddenly she opened her eyes wide. Yes, she thought, tomorrow I will pray not only to Athena and Artemis, but also to Poseidon. The god of the sea and of the winds loves Athens, too. Deriving great comfort from this plan, she quickly fell asleep.

Before dawn Tunnis gently awoke the girls and helped them to dress in warm woollen tunics and thick, soft woollen himations. She settled Rhode in her travelling chair, wrapping the hem of her himation snugly around her sandalled feet. Into both girls' hands she thrust some warm honey cakes with almonds. No one noticed that Epiktiti carried a basket of all her possessions, ready to leave Nyresa and begin her journey. The three set out, with the four slaves, in the dark of a cool September morning. They headed east towards the Acropolis, which, in daylight, they could see from Rhode's house.

After only a few minutes they joined a wide road that circled the Acropolis. Soon they had reached the Eleusinium, the shrine to Demeter and Persephone where Rhode had first met her well-born friend Agariste. Rhode knew that Nyresa and her grandmother wanted to stop to pray here. Nyresa had already told Rhode about her nightmares of earthquakes, volcanic eruptions and Hades, but she hadn't explained how truly frightening they were.

As the party climbed the stairs up to the Acropolis the sky was still dark blue, with only a suggestion of lapis lazuli brightening the horizon. Nyresa silently blessed her grandmother for taking her up the Sacred Rock, as the Acropolis was known. Every step up from the ground soothed her. I feel like I'm going home, her heart thrilled. The slaves, meanwhile, were grateful for Epiktiti's slow pace up the stairs. Upon entering the enclosure, the whole party stopped to survey the scene. Before them were two temples: to their left, a very old one enclosed by a stone fence and, to their right, a massive marble temple only just being built, a rectangle of roofless columns. White marble statues stood about the plateau, some lined up against the fortified walls that encircled the Rock, some along the paths, and some placed in the Acropolis's open spaces. Epiktiti walked slowly up the path between the two temples, leading the party to the Altar of Athena. She positioned herself behind the Altar, facing east, while Nyresa and Rhode came round to face her. The bearers gently placed Rhode's chair on the soil while Nyresa knelt on the ground beside her.

Just at that moment the sun rose, striking the pediment of the ancient temple, known as Athena Polias. Nyresa raised her eyes to gaze at the pediment in amazement. There she saw larger-than-life stone sculptures of Athena and Zeus battling the Giants. Athena's golden cape was made up of entwined, twisting snakes. Her helmet was decorated with small, coiled serpents. In her outstretched left hand she held the neck and head of a serpent uncoiling from the hem of her himation. Her face, as she battled an enormous giant, was sculpted beauty: serene, pale, with perfect, fine-cut features. My kore, Nyresa thought, electrified. She has the same expression, the same non-smile and calm of my kore!

Nyresa was stunned by the size, beauty and terror of the sculpted figures. On Thira she had seen nothing like this. She remembered what had happened in this Battle of the Giants: over a hundred giants were killed, some were tossed into the sea by the gods, others buried alive under the islands. The wrath of these buried giants brought earth-quakes and exploding mountains.

She remembered the yellow, gaseous bubbles rising from the caldera's depth and bursting on her hand. 'Oh, Athena,' she whispered. 'Protect me, goddess, and my island and the spirit of my mother.'

The sun rose higher, now striking the Altar, causing it to glow against the six elegant marble columns behind. Epiktiti raised her arms in salutation to the sun and began to chant a song to Athena in her deep, husky voice. Rhode might have been a marble statue beside Nyresa as she sat, motionless, so elegant she should not have been real. The chanting calmed Nyresa and she began gently to sway to her grand-mother's rhythm.

Epiktiti bowed to the sun, quietly praying to Apollo and thanking him for his protection. Then she turned and, nodding to the girls, began to walk back down the central path to the front western corner of the Acropolis. The bearers picked up Rhode's chair and followed. Epiktiti stopped at another altar, facing west, towards Phaleron and the Saronic Gulf. Nyresa knew this shrine, dedicated to Artemis, had been placed there by her worshippers from Brauron. Epiktiti drew from her basket a rounded pot with a short neck and two horizontal handles. Black figures of women offering wine were painted around its red terracotta sides. Carefully she uncorked it and solemnly poured red wine before the altar, beside it, and then slowly on to the altar, where it formed a blood-red pool, staining the marble. The rays of the newly risen sun turned the pool into glass, a mirror reflecting the dawn clouds in the sky above the Acropolis.

'Artemis, we thank you for our safe journey across the seas. We thank you for our loving family who have welcomed us in Athens and given Nyresa a home while I am on my pilgrimage. Protect them, I beg of you, from the Persians. Protect all of Athens, with the help of the great protector, the divine Athena, with the help of Zeus, father of all the gods, and with the help of your brother Apollo, the light of reason and justice. I beg you to beseech Poseidon, ruler of the seas, to release the winds imprisoned in Aeolus's sack. Turn them free to work their havoc on the Persian fleet, bound in the Thracian Sea. Lastly, I invoke the early kings of Athens, Erechtheus and Theseus, to watch over this city and my family.' The pool of wine spread towards the altar's edge and then began to drip on to the ground.

Slowly Epiktiti turned back to her basket and withdrew from it a small leather pouch. More slowly still, she upended the pouch, pouring what looked like a handful of stones into her palm. Nyresa held her breath. Epiktiti solemnly unrolled the stones, revealing a necklace, which she held up to the sun. Turning then to Nyresa, she held the necklace out to her. Nyresa and Rhode could see the round stones were of lovely pastel colours: white, grey, beige, blue. In the middle of the necklace, just where it would nestle in the hollow of a girl's throat, was a striped stone. It was magical.

Epiktiti approached Nyresa and placed the necklace around her neck. Nyresa put her hand to the necklace and felt the cool round, stone beads. She counted ten.

'This necklace, Nyresa, is made of the stones of Thira. It is very old and rare. Only women of Thira, of ancient families, have such necklaces, crafted before the volcano erupted. It has seen every age of Thira's history. Wear it proudly. Know it has been worn and loved for many generations, and will protect you for all time. This one has been in our family, passed down from each woman to her daughter, for hundreds of years. My mother gave it to me when I became a woman and I gave it to your mother when she became a woman. And now I pass it on to you.' She smiled into her granddaughter's eyes. 'You are nearly a woman, my darling. You are twelve and have danced the partheneion. Soon you will be a parthenos. You wear your hair loose now, but soon you will braid and bind it in the time-honoured fashion of girls of marriageable age.'

Straightening her stiff, old back, Epiktiti looked again into the rising eastern sun and whispered hoarsely, 'Artemis, protect these girls, these nymphs, no longer maidens. They face many trials and great danger.'

She turned again to the girls. 'I hope to go soon on my pilgrimage.' She looked gently at Nyresa; Rhode, too. 'Look after each other.' Epiktiti looked again into the sky. Then facing Nyresa, she leaned over her again and, taking her face into her hands, kissed both cheeks, both eyes, and her forehead. Just for a moment she pressed the girl's head to her heart. Then she approached Rhode and did the same. Without another word Epiktiti picked up her basket and preceded them along the path to the ancient portico.

Nyresa sat down on a stone bench alongside the

Acropolis's wall. In the early light, Rhode in her chair and Nyresa on the bench sat in silence, gazing over the western and southern areas of the city. Nyresa's left hand gently touched her ten beads, slipping them through her fingers again and again. All was silent as the city slept. Only a few people, quietly making their way along the streets, made any movement. After a while Rhode nodded to her porters, who picked up her chair and, with Nyresa following, slowly walked along the path out through the ancient portico to the wide platform at the head of the stairs. Epiktiti, motionless, was standing at the edge of the marble platform, facing Phaleron.

Nyresa scanned the horizon towards the sea, towards Phaleron. She could see nothing, no real movement, but suddenly she heard a distinct rumbling sound. Noise, movement, louder noise, came rolling towards them from the furthest houses. The sound grew, as if rolling forwards, and now they could make out people rushing and banging iron pots with spoons, yelling, shouting, screaming, pelting up and down the streets. A tidal wave of noise and movement rolled up from the port, gaining height and momentum as it rose up towards Athens. On the platform, Epiktiti, the girls and the bearers watched as silent, sleeping houses suddenly awoke to furious activity, spreading the noise. Then the wave swept up the Acropolis, crashed on the stairs, and overwhelmed them all.

'The Persians have turned back!'

'The Persians have gone!'

'Their ships broke up at the headland of Mount Athos! Three hundred ships have been destroyed.'

'Mardonius has been wounded! He may be dying.'

'Twenty thousand men have drowned! They fell from their ships, they were eaten by sharks, the waves dashed their bodies on rocks.'

'The cold water and the northerly gale killed them!'

'The Brygi tribe in Macedonia attacked their camp!'

'They've turned back. They're retreating!'

'The Persians are gone.'

'We're safe. Safe for another year!'

On and on went the shouting as the news spread through the galvanized city.

The cousins clasped each other for joy, tears streaming down their faces. Nyresa found it hard to breathe, only now aware of how frightened she had been; hard to see through her tears; hard to hear for the turmoil. She rushed to the end of the platform and strained to see the city below, to see the people as they spread the word. Everywhere she looked there was tumult. No normal sound could be heard for the din. The rejoicing was so great she felt it in her bones. She looked down to the right and saw the Agora filling up with men, women and children. People were scrambling up the steps in front of the Acropolis, to the rocky plateau of the Areopagus. Even on Thira she had heard of the rock on which sat the famed Areopagus, the Council of Athens. Today there would be no Council. Today, as Mardonius and his surviving forces headed home to Persia, the Athenian people clambered on to the rock's broad hump, yowling with glee in the early morning light and shaking their fists against the streaked skies.

Then Nyresa ran back to Rhode and asked her – she had to shout it – 'Rhode, how many people live in Athens?'

Her cousin looked surprised for a second but turned her head to Nyresa and shouted back, 'Five hundred thousand, father once told me!'

Nyresa was amazed. Slowly she turned again to look over the city. Everywhere she looked within the circular city wall there was noise and joyous commotion. Beyond the wall, though, lay a vast, still plain, eventually sloping up into the encircling mountains. Athens, she thought to herself, is like a pearl in the middle of a shallow drinking vessel. So different from Thira, a marble mountain perch overlooking vast seas.

She suddenly realized her grandmother had vanished. Nyresa leaned towards Rhode and shouted, 'My grandmother! She's gone. I'll look in the temple!' Before Rhode could reply, she dashed across the platform, back under the ancient portico.

She hurried up the middle path, straight up through the two temples, past the Altar of Athena, up and up to the very eastern end of the plateau. Standing there, she looked in all directions. The wind had risen with the morning, blowing her himation and tunic and hair every which way. Where was her grandmother? Then she realized where she had to go. She scurried back down the path and strode straight into the ancient temple of Athena.

She marched quickly, without looking up, right beneath the frieze of Athena and Zeus battling the Giants. Inside the eastern chamber, the inner sanctum of the temple, all was silence, gloom and flickering torchlight. No sounds of rejoicing could be heard here, only the beating of her own heart. What she saw first was a glimmer of gold, then her eyes made out the seated statue of Athena, against a stone screen, the olivewood Athena, ancient, known to have fallen from the sky. The goddess was adorned with gold: a gold diadem, gold necklaces, a gold cloak and a gold owl on her shoulder. The temple's eastern chamber was divided into three aisles by rows of pillars. Torches, held in high iron sconces on the walls, gave out a thin, flickering light.

Nyresa knelt and then prostrated herself in front of the goddess. Only she and Athena were in the eastern chamber. Through the stone wall dividing the temple, she heard her grandmother's deep voice chanting songs of thanks to Poseidon–Erechtheus, honoured in the western chamber. The sea! Nyresa remembered her grandmother had prayed to Artemis to ask Poseidon to bring the winds to sink the Persian ships.

She slipped out of the temple and joined her grandmother, already walking along the path between the temples. With Epiktiti's arm around her shoulder, they walked together through the Acropolis, towards the ancient portico. Nyresa knew that, with the Persian threat gone, her grandmother would want to leave soon, but she had not realized *how* soon. Her grandmother turned to embrace her, then descended the marble stairs and the dirt path, disappearing through the portico. Suddenly Nyresa realized her grandmother had begun her pilgrimage. Nyresa was alone.

III

Zeus realized that if all human beings died, there would be no one to worship the gods. He sent a message to Hades begging him to return Persephone to her mother. Then Zeus sent a message to Demeter saying that she could have her daughter back on the single condition that she had not yet tasted the food of the dead.

Hades hid his anger and lied to Persephone, his reluctant bride, telling her that as she was so unhappy in the Underworld with him, he had decided to send her home to her mother. Persephone, overjoyed, leapt into the chariot of Hermes, the messenger god. But just as they were about to leave, one of Hades' gardeners ran over to the chariot hooting with laughter and shouting. He told Hades that he had watched Persephone in the orchard and had seen her eat seven seeds of the pomegranate from a tree there.

Persephone paled. Panic made her dizzy. She remembered the day she had eaten those seeds, wandering in the murky, cheerless palace grounds of Hades. It wasn't her fault she had eaten them. She had been tricked! Her mother would be so angry. But the seeds had been eaten, as surely as Hades had abducted her, as surely as he had taken her to his home.

DANGER

492 BC

1. FAR FROM HOME

It was a month since the city's reprieve and Epiktiti's departure. Klio, the flute player, was walking through the Agora thinking how she had been in Athens almost exactly a year. A year ago her life had been different. She had just turned fourteen and been promised in marriage to the son of a taverna keeper. But her home island, Aegina, was in turmoil, unsafe, and her parents and the parents of her fiancé thought it best to remove her to Athens until life at home settled down.

How can life at home settle down? she asked herself for the millionth time. Aegina was hopelessly entwined in war. Sparta had tried to invade, then Athens had accused Aegina of collaborating with the Persians. Aegina's location was the problem. The island lay directly in front of Athens' port, in the middle of the Saronic Gulf. Aegina would indeed be the perfect jumping-off place for a Persian or Spartan invasion.

Klio hated being apart from her fiancé in spite of the excitement of Athens. Living here with her guardian, Gorgo, she had few friends of her own age and she often wondered how her homeland had changed, and whether her fiancé missed her too. She smiled sadly to remember meals she and her parents had had at the taverna when everything seemed simple and right. She sighed. She didn't mind being hired to play her flute as she had always expected to work; she just knew by now, ordinarily, she'd have been married and had a child, as her Aeginetan friends her age had.

When Klio reached the Agora she wandered lazily among its stalls and her mood brightened. After all, she had much to be thankful for. Aegina had not yet been attacked, she loved her guardian, she had established an excellent reputation as a flute player in Athens, and Mardonius had now returned to Persia. If only all this added up to her being able to return to Aegina. She was already fifteen, rather old not to be married and a mother. Instead, I spend all my time trying to avoid the amorous advances of my clients when I play at their symposias, she thought. She pulled herself together, straightening her back and shoulders. Enough remembering, she ordered herself.

Then she noticed the dark-haired girl Cherson had been so taken with a few weeks ago, standing across the Agora and carrying a caged pigeon. Klio had promised Cherson she would introduce herself to this girl – and casually tell her about him. She observed Nyresa carefully.

Nyresa had come to the Agora because Rhode had asked her to – she needed someone to run an errand for Agariste. Nyresa had to find out if the robins had arrived, an annual invasion that delighted all Athenians. Suddenly, always in October, the month of Boedromion, the sky and trees magically filled with noisy, red-breasted birds. Nyresa was to carry one of Agariste's pigeons to the Agora and, once she'd discovered whether the robins had arrived, remove the pigeon from its wicker cage, fix a message to its leg and loose it to return to Agariste. The pigeon was young and untested, and the message it would deliver, though delightful, was less important than the delivery.

Nyresa took on the favour for her cousin with little enthusiasm. She had had many friends in Thira who kept pigeons, but she had never cared much for them herself. She didn't like their constant conversation or their droppings. Dribbling at both ends was how she thought of them. Nyresa sighed. All right, bird, she thought, I shall look out for the robins and then I'll send you off.

Nyresa had pushed her way along the corridors between the fruit and vegetable stalls. First she made her way past the stalls piled with squashes of different shapes and hues. Then she passed tables laden with red peppers, green peppers, yellow peppers and mushrooms, some as large as a plate, some smaller than her fingertip. Pushing her way through the crowds, down another passage, this one well covered by brightly striped awnings, she gazed with wonder at the fruits – baskets and huge terracotta platters, full of different varieties.

She was standing staring at these fruits when she was approached by a girl who looked strangely familiar: very pretty, with sparkling warm eyes.

'Hello,' said the pretty stranger.

Nyresa was embarrassed and flattered, and a little startled. 'Hello.'

'I didn't mean to scare you. I saw you about a month ago in the Agora and just wanted to meet you.' Klio had a disarmingly gentle yet straightforward manner.

Nyresa was mesmerized by Klio; never had she seen such a beautiful girl. Glyka was pretty and merry, and Rhode tranquil and lovely. This girl reminded Nyresa of poured honey. She had golden brown hair and large, limpid brown eyes, with dark lashes. Her white teeth were perfect, her skin creamy and gilded by the sun, enlivened by sudden blushes. What most drew Nyresa's gaze was the unutterable sweetness emanating from her face and gently expressed in her manner and bearing. She held her raised arm with a dancer's grace. Every gesture of her hands was lovely, eye-catching in its beauty.

'Oh! Yes,' Nyresa answered, embarrassed to remember which Agora visit that probably was. The one with Tunnis. Nyresa blushed to think how stupid she must have looked, being dragged around the Agora on that first tour. I must be braver, she commanded herself. I must be more like Glyka . . . Of course. Glyka, that's who she reminds me of! Nyresa immediately looked up into Klio's face and smiled. 'I would like to meet you, too.'

Soon the girls were talking about everything as they sauntered about the Agora. Nyresa heard about Klio's fiancé and Gorgo and Klio's flute playing at symposia. Klio heard about Thira and Glyka, and how Nyresa had to leave to live in Athens while her grandmother was on her pilgrimage. Nyresa even told Klio about her necklace.

'I miss my grandmother a lot,' Nyresa confided.

'Sometimes I just lie on my bed and roll the beads of my necklace around and around my neck. I like Rhode very much and I am glad I've got to know her, but I still miss my life on Thira.'

'I know exactly what you mean,' Klio said warmly. 'I have a whole circle of friends here in the Agora. I love them all and never would have known them had I stayed in Aegina. Still . . .'

'Tell me about your friends,' Nyresa said with interest. 'I know so few people because my cousin –' She broke off, ashamed to seem to be blaming Rhode for the limitations of her life. It was true Rhode could not go out and had had to let most of her friendships wither. Still, that was hardly her fault, Nyresa reminded herself.

'My best friend is, of course, my guardian, Gorgo,' Klio said earnestly. 'She is the most loving, attentive guardian a person could have.' Klio grew solemn. 'She is called the Fate of the Agora because people say she has magical powers. She is very close to being blind but sits spinning in the same place every day, in the Agora. People compare her to Clotho, the Fate who spins a thread for each person's life.'

'Has she ever cut a thread and killed someone?' Nyresa whispered.

'No,' Klio answered. 'I don't think she *is* Clotho, but she is very wise and seems to know more than most. I think her predictions as well as her sightless eyes scare people.'

'Where does she sit?' Nyresa asked, as much for something neutral to say as to be sure to know where not to go. The whole idea of Gorgo made her apprehensive.

'She always sits at the bend of the Panathenaian Way, which is the main road that cuts through the Agora to the Acropolis. She sits beside the little girls who weave the peplos – you know, the cloak – which the statue of Athena in the ancient temple will wear during the Panathenaea, the birthday festival we hold every year for the goddess. You've missed it for this year. But you'll be here for it next summer, won't you?'

Nyresa gloomily nodded her head.

Klio hurried on to a safer topic, one that she hoped would distract and interest Nyresa. 'My best friend is a boy named Cherson – and I caught him watching you!' Her expression had changed entirely and now her eyes twinkled with good humour.

Nyresa, though, blushed with embarrassment and alarm and Klio was immediately sorry. Trying to make amends, she began prattling about her other Agora friends, especially the cobbler and his welcoming shop, and then a little more about Cherson. The last thing Klio said made everything perfect: 'As you get to know everyone, you will be able to tell Rhode lots of stories. Together, we can gather all the gossip of Athens for her!'

The two girls made plans to meet the next day at the fruit stall where they'd first met. As they parted, Nyresa headed for the clump of plane trees by the monument to the Eponymous Heroes. If robins were arriving today, surely they'd come here, she thought. As she threaded her way through the crowds in the Agora, she thought: I like it here; I like the excitement and the bustle and all the different people. She glanced sideways at the Acropolis and, for the first time, didn't feel that twist in her stomach, the longing for home.

2. A BOY

Nyresa made her way to the monument to the Eponymous Heroes and gratefully sat down on the now familiar stone bench beneath the clump of trees. As she did so she let her baskets half tumble on to the ground, much to the consternation of Agariste's pigeon. She let her hands fall into her lap and, composed, began to search the skyline for robins. First she looked past the monument, then over the roofs of the government buildings – one in a beehive shape, which she liked, called the Tholos, and a second, more traditional building with columns, the Bouleuterion. In the distance she could see the tree-covered slope, the Kolonos Agoratos. Her gaze tarried on the slope, for Klio had told her that the boy Cherson lived and worked in a blacksmith's house there. Above the slope she stared at the marble outcrop of the Acropolis. She never ceased to marvel at the massive stone wall built along the outer edge of its plateau.

Then, as if out of nowhere, a boy was before her, grinning. A rather handsome boy, and one who had clearly been at the sports ground, for he was wearing the simplest tunic and had a flask of exercising oil suspended from his wrist. Nyresa forgot completely about the robins.

'I'm called Cherson,' the youth smiled, enjoying Nyresa's consternation. 'But my real name is Ajax,' he said. Then he paused, clearly waiting for Nyresa to ask him why he had two names.

She didn't ask, however, but instead just watched him in silence.

This silence Cherson found irritating. 'All right. I'll tell you.'

Nyresa was enjoying herself. So this was the boy Klio had described.

Cherson ran his hand through his tight black curls. 'My story. I come from the Chersonese.' He saw a frown cross her face. 'That's a huge peninsula thrusting into the north Aegean, right between the Asian coast and Thrace.' Nyresa's frown smoothed. 'My great-uncle was once ruler there. When he died, my father became the ruler.'

'Why didn't your great-uncle's son become ruler?' Nyresa asked, following closely.

'Because my great-uncle didn't have any children. And his brother, my grandfather, was assassinated. So the throne passed to my father who was also killed.'

'Killed? Both of them? By whom?'

'Hippias and his family, the former tyrants of Athens. Now, though, my uncle is here in Athens and probably the most important commander of the Athenian army.' Nyresa sat back a little at that. 'His name is Miltiades.'

'But why are you and your uncle not in the Chersonese?'

'Because,' answered Cherson, not without condescension, 'last summer Mardonius and his army overran and occupied the Chersonese. The Persian emperor Darius controls it now.'

'Will you be ruler one day,' Nyresa asked, 'if the Persians are expelled, that is?'

Cherson's face clouded. 'Perhaps. If the gods will it. But there's a problem, you see. My mother and father weren't married. Officially I am not recognized as a member of my father's clan and, until I am, I can't inherit titles, property or rights.'

'Is your mother living?' Nyresa asked quietly.

Cherson looked away as he answered, as though speaking to a third person. 'She died two years ago. That was when I decided to come to Athens. It was my mother who gave me the name Ajax. Ajax, the hero of the Trojan War, was the founder of our family. That's his statue behind you, on the monument to the Eponymous Heroes.'

Nyresa looked solemnly at the statue, then back at Cherson-Ajax. He's an orphan, she thought, like me.

Cherson regained his smile, knowing she was thinking about his story. 'I have come to Athens to convince my uncle that I am truly his nephew and worthy of our clan. This I hope to do on the battlefield, when the Persians come. My uncle has long known about me – from the Chersonese but especially during these two years I've been in Athens – and sort of watches out for me. Thanks to him I'm allowed to attend the palaistra, where Athenian boys take classes and exercise. I have to split my time, though, between work at the blacksmith's and the palaistra.'

An unpleasant thought occurred to Nyresa. 'So you want there to be a war?'

He rose to lean against the tree. 'I want to be recognized

by my uncle, legally, officially. I can think of two ways to achieve this: glory on the battlefield or glory in the Olympics.'

Nyresa also rose and inadvertently knocked the wicker cage, causing Agariste's bird to squawk and scrabble. 'Oh, this bird! I forgot all about it – and the robins!'

Cherson looked down at the cage for a moment, then continued right on: 'I figure I have a good chance at the four-horse chariot race, the quadriga.' He puffed out his chest a bit, smiling complacently.

'You are a ridiculous boy,' Nyresa laughed.

'That's exactly what Klio calls me. Why am I so ridiculous? I do! My great-grandfather won the quadriga at the Olympics. My grandfather won the quadriga three times at the Olympics. And his brother won at the Olympics once. I love horses and I *am* very good with them, just ask the blacksmith. I want to enter the quadriga as soon as I can. I'm seventeen now. I'll try to enter the first time in a few years and I'll keep trying until I win. I want to be the most famous charioteer in Greece.'

Just as Nyresa was about to tease Cherson for his conceit, an astonishing thing happened. The sky turned black, as in a sudden storm, and there were robins everywhere. Hundreds, thousands of robins! They were in the trees chirping, on the ground strutting, hopping from the fence around the monument to the ground, flapping up to the benches. Nyresa looked over at the stalls and saw the birds walking along the tables, stealing food, some resting on the stalls' canopies. Everyone in the Agora stopped and laughed, delighted to see the robins return. Nyresa and Cherson smiled happily.

Rapidly Nyresa got a strip of linen and a piece of charcoal out of one of her baskets. Stretching the cloth on her thigh, she wrote a short message, swooped down upon the pigeon in its basket, tied the cloth around its ankle with string, and grabbed it firmly about its wings and body. She then walked from the monument into the centre of the Agora and, finding a patch of empty space, flung it straight up into the air. Disorientated and cross at this treatment, the pigeon nearly fell back into her hands. But then nature asserted itself, the pigeon remembered it was a pigeon and off it flew, eager to get back to its home.

Cherson watched with interest. There was something determined about this girl. He liked that. What he said, however, was, 'Aren't these robins astounding? Now I've seen them twice. But your pigeon – what is all that about?'

'Oh,' she gave a little embarrassed laugh, 'my cousin's friend wanted word sent to her when the robins returned to the Agora.'

He liked the way her face changed expression so quickly, like clouds blowing rapidly across the sky. Her dark hair hung in ringlets and curls around her face and down to her shoulders. She was a pretty girl. 'And why doesn't the friend come see for herself? Or your cousin, whose friend she is?' he asked.

These questions made Nyresa a little cross, though she wasn't sure why. They seemed somehow intrusive. 'My cousin is lame and can hardly walk. And her friend is an

Athenian lady, not meant to mix among crowds.' Nyresa picked up her baskets and turned to the boy. 'Goodbye, Cherson-Ajax.'

'Goodbye? But I told you my life story and I haven't heard anything of yours. Where are you from? Why are you in Athens?' He saw her face darken and quickly changed tack. 'I've seen you before. I saw you with my friend Klio just now. And before. It was about a month ago. You were being dragged around the Agora by a rhinoceros.'

That did it. 'Tunnis is not a rhinoceros! She is loving and trustworthy and decent and kind. And if Rhode didn't have her, I don't know what she'd do because her mother hardly cares for her one bit, hardly even thinks of her. She is ashamed to have a crippled daughter. And all her father cares about is business. Her parents completely ignore her!'

Cherson quickly retreated. 'I didn't mean to upset you. I didn't even mean to be rude about "Tunnis", is it? Please forgive me.'

Though genuinely alarmed at the hole he'd dug for himself, Cherson was also acting a part, well aware, Nyresa thought, of the effect of his pleading, brown eyes. Boys are irritating, she thought, especially conceited boys. They think they can get away with anything. 'I forgive you,' was all she would give him. 'Goodbye.'

'But wait,' Cherson said quickly. 'Can't we meet again? I could show you the Pynx – that marble hill up there. I bet you've never been there.' He pointed to a nearby hillside. Nyresa looked up at it and was perplexed: the hill was covered in deep forest except for one side that was treeless and shiny. She looked more closely. The open space was an enormous outcrop of marble into which rows of benches had been carved. 'That's where the Assembly meets – all the citizens of Athens. They debate and argue there, and make laws and vote. It's fun to see when it's empty, too. We could walk up there one day.'

Nyresa looked closely at Cherson. Was it appropriate for a girl to walk up the hillside with a boy? If she were younger and on Thira it would be fine. But she had danced the partheneion. 'If Klio wants to visit the Pynx, that would be fun,' she answered and walked away.

3. FISH AND SANDALS

On the way home Nyresa thought of her friends, old and new. Klio was made to leave Aegina and her fiancé, to live without her family in Athens. Cherson was orphaned, left his home in the Chersonese, and was still unrecognized by his family. Next summer Glyka would leave Thira to live in a colony along the African coast. Even Rhode was bereft, in a way, stuck at home with no one thinking about her and no prospect of marriage. Everyone's lives seemed surrounded with sadness and uncertainty.

When she got home and entered Rhode's wing of the house, Nyresa found Tunnis just clearing away two elegant tea glasses. There was a guilty look about the slave.

Puzzled, Nyresa asked, 'Who has been here, Tunnis?'

Tunnis kept her face turned down. Rhode called her from the patio. 'Nyresa, I'm out here.'

'Who has been here, Rhode?' Nyresa repeated.

'Agariste,' Rhode answered.

'But why wasn't I told? You know I've never met her and have always wanted to.' Then Nyresa grew quiet. 'Was that why I was sent out to the Agora to watch for the robins? To get me out of the house?'

Pink suffused Rhode's neck and climbed to her cheeks. 'Nyresa, I'm sorry. I have been sworn to secrecy and cannot tell you anything.' Although clearly ashamed, she remained composed and set. Nyresa gazed back for a moment, dropped the birdcage on the patio floor, and left for her own bedroom.

Weeks passed. The frostiness between Nyresa and Rhode saddened them both but wouldn't thaw. Rhode would not speak and Nyresa was furious. Over these early winter months when Tunnis asked Nyresa to go to the Agora, Nyresa grabbed her baskets and ran out of the house.

Today Tunnis had sent her to the cobbler's shop with a pair of her uncle's sandals that needed repair. She hadn't yet been to the cobbler's shop and had forgotten it was one of Klio's favourite places. She had not seen much of Klio over the past weeks – and Cherson not at all. But today, miserable but confident, Nyresa strode along the narrow streets under the shadow of the Acropolis towards the Agora. It was cold so she'd wrapped herself up well, with two himations – one around her shoulders, dropping to her ankles, and one around her neck and head, falling on top of the first one. She also wore socks with calf-length boots. A light snow was falling, which ordinarily she loved, but she took no pleasure in it today.

Although Nyresa hadn't been to every shop and stall in the Agora, or encountered every poet, philosopher, mystic, or politician who conversed there, she knew her way around. She strode into the cobbler's shop and he looked up, surprised at the sudden entry. He smiled to see the pretty young foreign girl with her determined expression. Her black curls had crept out from the cream-coloured himation and encircled her fresh, rosy-cheeked face. 'Could it be sandals you want repairing?' he asked with a smile.

'Yes, thank you,' she replied primly, firmly placing her uncle's sandals on the cobbler's counter.

The cobbler took each sandal in his strong, calloused hands, turning it over, gently pulling at various thongs, studying the soles. Nyresa sneaked a look at him and saw a big, friendly-looking, middle-aged man with rough skin on his face, black hairs coming out of his nose and ears, and terrible, torn, jagged fingernails. His thumbs were bashed and lumpy – from his hammers, Nyresa guessed. She frowned to think about this last detail but decided she liked him, even if his appearance was a bit frightening. His shop was warm and had a wonderful smell. She looked about and saw several clay braziers, one with a shallow, covered stewpot on top. She was also astonished to see a portable clay oven nearby.

The cobbler quickly glanced at Nyresa and chuckled. 'Oh, yes, all the comforts of home I have here. You see my dinner and my bread cooking? I'm here all the hours the gods give us so I figure I might as well enjoy them. And my shop stays warm!' They exchanged a comfortable smile and the friendship was sealed.

With the sound of the charcoal crackling and sometimes tumbling its short way down to the clay base, and the gentle bubbling of the stew, the shop soothed Nyresa and transported her into a fine, dreamy mood. Nothing smells as good as baking bread. She forgot her grumpiness and any desire for haste. The cobbler, especially happy to have this pleasant young girl to talk to, began to tell stories about his favourite topic.

'Do you see these sandals?' he asked, waving his arm up and across the width of the room, indicating a wall of shelves holding pair after pair of sandals. She nodded, obligingly. 'They come from all over the world!'

Nyresa looked up and cast her eyes over all the shoes on the shelves. She saw lacy, leather-soled sandals with what looked like cobwebs of thongs. She saw elegantly tooled sandals, elaborately decorated with embossed patterns, each raised surface brightly coloured with blue or green or red paint. There were knee-high boots, soft, with criss-cross lacings, and mid-calf ones, sturdy, made out of tough leather. Some ladies' sandals she saw had to be only for display, they were so delicate, with such thin soles. A mere thong ran up from the sole and around the big toe, or up between two toes and connecting at the ankle to another thong. She saw soldiers' sandals stuck with hobnails in the soles and other military ones that looked like leather socks. She saw men's sandals of thick, bold thongs that strapped across the foot and around the lower leg. Everyone was represented here, she thought.

Seeing how and where each pair was ragged or worn touched her heart. The man who owns those sandals must come down hard on his heels, being forthright, she thought. The lady who owns those high-priced delicate sandals has worn them hard: she needs less grand, sturdier ones. A poor soldier must own the pair next to hers, with its many gashes and holes. Where have his sandals been? In battle, of course, and in rain and snow and freezing sleet. Our sandals tell our stories, Nyresa thought ... Suddenly she checked herself, remembering Rhode with her pairs of pristine sandals, never dirty or wet, worn only on the inside edges, from the slow pulling of one foot after the other.

The cobbler looked over the shoes proprietorially, proudly. 'They say one has to walk in the sandals of a man to understand him. Walk in these sandals and you'll understand not just Athenians and Corinthians and Spartans, but Egyptians, Lydians, Thracians, Etruscans, even –' here he paused dramatically, 'Persians!'

Nyresa was astonished. 'Persian sandals? Here?'

'Oh, yes,' he bragged. 'Everyone comes to me for repair.'

She turned a worried face up to the cobbler. She dropped her eyes and stepped back a little from the counter.

The cobbler saw she was worried. 'There are deep, dark secrets in the Agora. But if you want to learn them, just turn your head to the right and look out of my window.'

She turned with trepidation. Through the window she

saw the fish stall, with its short queue of wealthy patrons. She remembered Rhode had also told her about the fish queue.

'The people in that queue run this city or will determine its fate. Mark them well, young miss. Who is celebrating? Who looks sad, preoccupied?' He spoke in a stage whisper: 'Who is plotting? Consider where these people get the money for their expensive delicacies. Oh yes, the fish stall is an excellent place for discovering secrets.'

Nyresa turned a bewildered face to the cobbler.

'Do you not see?' he continued, looking with hard, cold eyes at the fish eaters. 'Such a person is called an *opsophagos* – an opson eater, a relish eater, a fish lover. They indulge their appetites for the most expensive food in Athens. Their appetites dominate their minds and hearts. Who knows what ideals these people have betrayed in their greed!' A hardness momentarily set his kindly features.

Nyresa thought she liked him, but he was definitely odd. 'What do you mean? They're just buying fish.' She looked earnestly into his face then quickly dropped her gaze, as girls are taught.

'Yes, yes,' he answered, suddenly subdued, looking now into the middle distance rather than at the queue. 'Some day you will understand.' His voice trailed off. Then he grew animated again. 'Do you see that man, the one first in line? That is Themistocles, the most important of the three chief magistrates who govern Athens. He's a deep one, he is. He's been arguing with the Assembly for years. He wants us to build up our navy – as if we could ever compete with the

Persian fleet! Look at the man behind him,' the cobbler continued. 'Always notice who's talking to whom in that queue. The man behind is cleverly trying to get on Themistocles's good side. Perhaps he's a friend of Themistocles's enemy, Aristides, and is digging for dirt.'

Nyresa stared obediently, trying to memorize each face.

'Mark my words,' the cobbler warned, 'whoever's in the fish queue has an appetite for something, and that makes him dangerous. Maybe he wants power? Maybe money?'

'Maybe fish?' Nyresa couldn't help but add, teasingly.

The cobbler burst out laughing. 'All right, maybe fish. I admit eating fish is a pleasure. Not everyone in the queue wants the biggest fish, the costliest. Most will have come for little fish like sprats, or salt fish, like tuna or mackerel. Nevertheless, my impertinent little friend, I'm telling you, there aren't that many big fish in the sea and there aren't that many big fish in Athens, either. You watch that fish queue to see who our big fish are, to see who wants power, even at the hands of the Persians. Men can be bought, just like fish. The bigger they are, the more expensive. Just you watch.'

Nyresa didn't fully understand, not the bit about excessive appetites and ideals – but she knew what the cobbler meant about men being buyable, like fish, and it worried her. She turned again to look out of the window just as Themistocles walked away. Then she caught sight of a very pretty woman, who looked like an elegant Athenian lady. The lady spoke momentarily with Themistocles, who was smiling and nodding, clearly flattered. Her face wasn't covered, which shocked Nyresa; an Athenian lady's face should be covered. And she shouldn't be talking, really, in public, especially to a man. Even if the man were her husband or brother, she wouldn't address him in public. Nyresa turned to ask the cobbler but he, having seen her wondering gaze and the object of her surprise and curiosity, quickly turned away and again began examining her uncle's sandals.

4. FATE

Before Nyresa could speak, Klio came into the shop, accompanied by an old woman whose uncertain steps and upturned face suggested blindness: Gorgo, the Fate of the Agora. Nyresa quickly studied her, and gave Klio a wide, happy smile.

'Nyresa,' Klio exclaimed, equally pleased. She hadn't seen as much of her new Thiran friend as she had hoped. She'd been busy over the autumn and early winter playing her flute at symposia. Such performances could earn her two, sometimes three, obols an evening. As the average wage for a day of hard physical labour for a man was six obols, Klio considered herself well paid.

'You've found your way to our good friend's shop,' she smiled while embracing the rough-hewn cobbler.

'Careful! You'll hurt yourself on my hammers, Klio,' he laughed, giving her a little hug back. Beaming at her with avuncular pride, he patted his leather apron, settling back into its pockets his hammers and long needles. 'So you know each other,' he said, pleased and surprised. 'This young lady came into my shop not half an hour ago. We've been peeking at the fish queue.' Klio started to laugh, and the cobbler turned to Gorgo. 'Gorgo,' he said, bowing and making a great sweep of his arm. 'May I present to you –' He suddenly stopped and looked at Nyresa. 'By the god of night, I must be sleeping! What *is* your name, my dear?' he asked.

'Nyresa,' she said shyly, keeping her eyes lowered, her dark curls hanging like bunches of grapes around her down-turned face. Everyone smiled. 'Nyresa of Thira,' she elaborated.

'May I present Nyresa of Thira? And Nyresa, may I present to you Gorgo, my long-standing friend, guardian of Klio, expert spinner and weaver – and sage! Klio, the best aulos player in Athens, you already know.' Introductions completed, he sat happily and gratefully upon his work stool, enjoying his assembled friends.

'Excuse me,' Nyresa said hesitantly. 'May I ask what *your* name is?'

The cobbler laughed. 'Everyone just calls me the cobbler. We all know who we mean, and it advertises my shop, so it suits me fine.'

Nyresa was aware that all this time Gorgo had said nothing. Her expression hardly gave clues to her thoughts or reactions, though it was intelligent and seemed acutely attentive. Nyresa's eyes silently appealed to Klio for help.

Klio had noticed her guardian start suddenly as she'd helped her over the threshold into the shop. It was as though her guardian had recognized Nyresa. She watched Gorgo's face and knew she was thinking rapidly. What could she be thinking? Her guardian was famous for her wisdom and predictions.

'Please, everyone; please join me in my feast of bread and stew.' The cobbler arranged short wooden work stools in a circle around the brazier, and took the bread out of its portable oven, allowing it to cool.

Gorgo turned her face towards Nyresa. Wrapped in a soft, luminously coloured himation that seemed to billow about her shoulders, she did seem something divine. Her eyes, whose irises were the light blue of the noon sky in summer, were ringed by a whiteness. The old woman gently smiled: 'Welcome to Athens, Nyresa. Klio has told me about you.'

Nyresa smiled politely while the cobbler began deftly serving up portions of stew and bread in little bowls for each guest. Although a mood of quiet settled on the group, the two girls actually were a bit nervous. Klio hoped her guardian would like her new friend and Nyresa, generally feeling bereft of friends since her fight with Rhode, wanted to make a good impression. The cobbler seemed simply happy in his hospitality.

Gorgo again turned to Nyresa, saying, 'I am not wholly blind, my dear. I can see some things, those worth seeing; like your wonderful beads. Did your mother give them to you?'

'In a way,' Nyresa bravely replied. 'My grandmother, who had once given them to my mother, gave them to me.'

She looked defiantly into the sightless blue eyes and suddenly felt ashamed and abashed, for she saw no hostility there, only kindness. Embarrassed, Nyresa turned away.

'Your mother named you "near the Acropolis" and here you are,' Gorgo continued.

The cobbler, Klio noticed, shot a quick, inquiring look at Gorgo. The steaming stew and fresh bread sat untouched in the bowls.

Gorgo began gently to rock. Nyresa's heart tightened as she remembered how Epiktiti used to rock as she spoke. 'Nyresa, it is no accident that you and Klio have met. Many times I have told our good friend the cobbler that the day would come when the young people of Greece would band together to serve Athens, that its fate lay in their hands.'

No one spoke. Gorgo was alarming both girls. Klio knew her guardian to be mysterious at times, but never had she heard her make such a bold, unexpected pronouncement. She didn't know what to think. Nyresa, already anxious in a variety of ways, was mesmerized by this strange old woman. She wanted both to leave and to stay.

Gorgo turned to Klio. 'You will be crucial in these matters, my dearest girl, because of your gentleness and loving heart. You will do what no one else can do. But to you, Nyresa,' she continued, turning her sightless face, 'to you will fall the hardest task. Your risk will be great; much will depend upon your bravery.'

Nyresa glared at Gorgo, as though trying to hold her at bay. Alarm coursed through her body. The hardest task, great risk, bravery? Leaving Thira had been all those things.

What else? What now? The old woman, like a falcon fixated on its prey, stared with unblinking white-ringed blue eyes at Nyresa.

A burst of deep-throated laughter broke the spell. Just outside the shop a pretty lady – the very lady Nyresa had been watching a few minutes ago – was speaking familiarly with a well-dressed man.

'They too will be part of your story,' Gorgo quietly said.

The cobbler nodded, keeping a careful eye as the pretty woman, accompanied by her servant, turned from the well-dressed, laughing man.

The two girls stared as though in a stupor at the woman.

Gorgo spoke. 'She is an hetaera.' Nyresa looked perplexed but Klio dropped her eyes. 'She is not a lady. Though she wears elegant clothes and lives grandly, she is *not* respectable. Athenian gentlemen dine in one of three places: at home with their wives; at symposia, where issues of the day are discussed with other men, and where dancers, singers, and flute players like Klio entertain; and at the home of an hetaera, where their hostess is beautiful, amusing and clever, and of questionable morals. The gentlemen are flattered to be invited – and they invite these women in turn to their symposia; they are the only sort of woman ever allowed to attend the symposia as guests. Klio has often seen hetaeras. They live by wealthy men giving them gifts. The cobbler and I have long been aware of this particular one. She is ambitious and untrustworthy. Mark her well. She is dangerous.'

Klio was embarrassed by her guardian's speech. She

wanted to signal to Nyresa that she felt the same way as Nyresa now looked: uneasy and apprehensive. What was all this talk of danger, bravery and hard tasks? Then a little comfort occurred to Klio. She pulled from her bag a small packet of honey dough balls and gave one to Nyresa.

Mechanically, Nyresa accepted. The honey burst in her mouth and ran down the back of her throat. The taste made her long for Glyka, for her grandmother, for Thira itself. The world of Athens was growing much too mysterious and threatening.

IV

When Demeter heard about the seven pomegranate seeds her daughter had eaten, she collapsed in misery.

Persephone would have said anything to undo her mistake. She remembered her mother's warnings the day she had gone to the fields; how frustrating she had found her mother's constant fears. Then she remembered the one scarlet poppy, the tallest, fullest, most inviting blossom she had been straining to pluck when Hades grabbed her. How beautiful and desirable it was in her mind – still. But now and forever when she thought of her mother, she saw in her face grief and loss. She knew that her mother was suffering, and she felt empty and sad.

Persephone would have to stay in the Underworld. Now all the earth was dry as dust, a wilderness of thorns. Demeter vowed she would never lift her curse or set foot on Olympus for the rest of eternity.

TREASON

491 BC

1. PERSEPOLIS

Half a world away the emperor Darius sat in his palace of Persepolis, receiving tribute from his provinces. The territory Darius controlled was nearly seventy times as vast as that of the Greeks. The procession before him of followers bringing gifts would take five full days to finish.

Thousands of men gathered in the palace. A sparrow had flown into the Council Hall, though no one had noticed. The bird was twenty metres up, flying about the carvings on the Hall's huge and heavily ornate capitals. Suddenly a whole flock of sparrows flew in, perhaps thirty or forty of them, again completely unobserved by the snaking procession below.

When Darius became emperor, he divided his lands into twenty provinces called satrapies. This week, all twenty satrapies were represented, offering luxurious gifts to the emperor. Ten thousand men, brilliantly dressed in tribal costumes, processed through the Council Hall. Two thousand men had passed by the emperor each day. From sun-up to sunset the slaves quickly and efficiently relieved the presenters of their gifts, recorded and stored them. By the end of this, the fifth day, all ten thousand would have processed.

Darius had sat, still as a statue, for four and a half days. Each sunset he rose, clumsy with stiffness, and left the Hall for the private part of the palace. At sun-up he returned and sat, without comment, for the next twelve hours. Each morning his dressers arranged his heavy robe over his knees and around his shins, so that he exactly resembled a carved statue. In his left hand he held the symbol of his authority: the lotus flower and two buds. The last touch was for his major-domo to place the royal sceptre in his right hand, gently wedging its point into the stand before the foot-stool. Darius had sat like this, immobile, each day for the past four days.

Having placed the sceptre, the major-domo stepped back to observe the procession. Now came the entry of the Egyptians. In their sheer linen wraps with only a thin linen tunic below, they had frozen during their four-day wait, he remembered, smiling. Persia is different from Egypt. There is no Nile here. No warmth in winter, or tropical birds, or bright, stunning flowers. The major-domo was secretly amused to see the statue-like king approached by the Egyptians, shivering, desperately trying not to fumble their fine gifts of folded linen. Even walking backwards from his royal presence, they were so hunched over with cold they couldn't bow properly. Then came the Median tributaries, properly dressed for Persia with stiff woollen jackets, leather tunics, peaked hats covering the backs of their necks. Their lands lay just north of Persia and Darius had built there one of his palaces at Ecbatana. They were carrying thick woollen blankets, heavy gold torques. The major-domo gazed with pleasure at their warhorses in their jewelled bridles.

As the procession rolled on, the emperor remained perfectly still. His beard lay flat on his chest: four rows of curls alternating with straight strands, the ends perfectly cut to form a rectangle. He did not feel the weight of the crown on his head for it sat high up on his thick hair, itself combed in a helmet of curls. His gaze was stony, his body calm, at one with his surroundings and his spirit. His high brow and straight nose seemed perfectly sculpted. He had been chosen to rule by Ahura-Mazda, the god of heaven, he who struggles against the darkness.

The procession moved on. Now the Elamites were presenting live lion cubs, wriggling against their chests, to the emperor. Behind the Elamites the Assyrians came, herding beautiful, perfumed rams with massive horns curling back against their necks.

Darius barely noticed. His mind turned inwards. To rule my vast lands requires ruthlessness; this my father taught me. He who works for me I reward according to his work. He who does ill, I punish according to the ill he has done.

Perspiration trickled the short distance from the emperor's hairline to the top of his beard. Darius's fingers twitched as they clutched the sceptre. He was remembering the storm last summer that had destroyed his fleet, almost killing Mardonius. The Athenians boasted that their god

Poseidon sent that storm. How dare they! Ahura-Mazda was ten thousand times more powerful than their Poseidon.

Rocks of rage hurtled through Darius's mind. Anger ran down his spine. *He who does ill, I punish.*

2. SECRETS

A month or so after Gorgo had warned the girls of their future, the Spartans attacked Aegina. But there was no slaughter. The Aeginetans immediately gave up when they saw they were outnumbered. The two cities of Sparta and Aegina reached a truce and all Klio could hear, as she walked about the Agora, were rumours of war between Aegina and Athens. Many Athenians muttered that it would be good to crush Sparta as well.

One winter morning, Klio and Nyresa sat together before the cobbler's clay brazier and marvelled at the madness of the Greeks. How could they plot and war against each other when Persia, their common enemy, was arming for an attack?

The question struck Nyresa unexpectedly hard, for it reminded her of her coldness to Rhode. Since the day of Agariste's visit, Rhode had maintained a distance, though affection and warmth trembled just beneath her reserve. Are we not like the Greek cities, Nyresa chided herself, quarrelling while real danger lies outside?

Klio knew about their estrangement and had been pressing Nyresa for weeks to make it up. 'You trusted Rhode before the secret visit by Agariste,' she reminded Nyresa.

'And Rhode told you she was sworn to secrecy. Something of great significance must be at stake for Rhode to remain silent this long while.'

Nyresa felt the weight of Rhode's isolation, knowing her parents were inattentive. All she had was Tunnis, Nyresa, Agariste, and her pigeons. Now Nyresa rose, thanked Klio, and headed home to find Rhode. By the time she found her, curled up in a chair in her room, tears were rolling silently down Nyresa's cheeks.

'Oh, Rhode, I'm so sorry I've been angry. Please forgive me.'

The older girl rose from her seat and enveloped her cousin in both arms, whispering, 'Thank you, Nyresa. Thank you.'

Four weeks passed. Very early on a February morning Rhode called from the balcony where she kept her pigeons, 'Nyresa. Wake! My pigeon Myrtle has returned with news!'

Nyresa opened one eye to look sideways at Rhode. 'Please, cousin Rhode,' she droned sleepily, 'cover Myrtle up with a nice, warm cloth, and let us both go back to bed.'

'No! You haven't understood. He has news from Agariste. Agariste is visiting us today. Us! She specifically stated that she hoped we both would be in.' Rhode carefully watched the lump of blanket on the bed. At first there was no change, then a barely perceptible movement. A blowsy head of black curls, like those of a gorgon, rose up from the depths of the bedding.

'She did?'

'She did.'

Nyresa made the effort to turn her head to Rhode. Finally Nyresa was going to be let in on the secret. She pushed her bed covers aside and jumped on to the freezing stone floor. Squeaking at the cold, she leapt back into bed and whirled the covers back over herself.

'Nyresa! Get up. I know it's cold, but if Agariste is prepared to cross most of Athens to visit us, the least we can do is dress and receive her with hot tea and warm sesame cakes.'

'Don't fret, Rhode. I'm getting up,' Nyresa scowled. Actually she was very excited, almost too excited to show Rhode.

At mid-morning there was a knock at the door. Tunnis opened it and, with great dignity, led Agariste in, crossing over to Rhode's sitting room, adjacent to her bedroom, where the two cousins awaited their guest. As Agariste entered, Nyresa looked up to see a stunning sight: the perfect Athenian lady. In shyness Nyresa dropped her eyes and began studying Agariste from the feet upwards. Her sandals hardly seemed there, so fine and light were they. Her toes were pink, indicating that she'd been carried by porters through the snow, her feet wrapped in a heated woollen cloth. Her tunic was unlike any draped cloth Nyresa had ever seen. The undergarment was a cream-coloured film of sheerest linen. Over it was draped a second tunic of soft blue, gathered at one side, just below the knee, drawing the eye to the right. A third tunic lay over this, of lapis lazuli, loose from the shoulders but cut in such a way that it fell in folds, starting at her shoulders, cascading down her body, held high above the waist with a ribbon, and then falling down to her ankles. Along the hem of the garment were spangles of triangles and spirals of gold and midnight blue.

Coils of dark-brown braids tumbled over and around Agariste's shoulders and back, down to her waist. Secured into the braids on top of her head was a crown of polished wood, inlaid with gold in a meander pattern. She wore beautiful, old-fashioned earrings: blue discs engraved with spiralling circles of red, like those found carved into the capitals of columns. Around her throat was a red-and-green necklace. She had gold bracelets on her wrists and jewelled rings on her fingers. And she gave off the scent of summer flowers. She knew her power and stood in silence before Nyresa and Rhode, waiting until her presence had been acknowledged. She was confident, not arrogant. This is Athens I am looking at, Nyresa thought.

Some memory tugged at Nyresa's heart as she gazed at Agariste. What was it? Her face, her smile? Her face held, in perfect balance, serenity and solemnity. My kore. This is her face, Nyresa thought. Agariste felt the intensity of Nyresa's gaze and hesitated before speaking.

'Nyresa, I'm pleased to meet you at last,' she said softly. 'I have a very particular reason for wanting to speak to you. It was at my behest that Rhode kept our secrets from you. Please excuse her. When you hear what we say, you may perhaps better understand.'

The three sat around a small tripod table, inlaid with cedar and olive wood. Braziers burned brightly in all four

105

corners of the room. Oil lamps gave a soothing, magical aura. First the two good friends briefly exchanged news. Myrtle had done well on this freezing winter morning to get so quickly to Rhode. Having confirmed that Rhode still had a number of Agariste's pigeons, the two young women arranged that today Agariste would take home several more of Rhode's birds. This way they could carry on their discussion after the visit. Nyresa was only mildly interested in these arrangements.

Agariste now turned to Nyresa and spoke directly.

'Nyresa, my family clan, the Alcmaeonidae – Alc-mae-on-i-dae,' she repeated slowly, 'have been mortal enemies of the family of Hippias – the Pisistratidae clan – for many generations.' She smiled: 'Pi-sis-tra-ti-dae.' Nyresa nodded at the unfamiliar names and Agariste resumed her speech. 'During the last century the quarrel was about power, about who would rule Athens. Finally the last Pisistratidus was exiled from Athens and my uncle, Cleisthenes, became the undisputed ruler. He used his power to change Athens's government to make it more democratic. He gave each citizen and metic the right to vote. Athens has been governed by these reforms for twenty years: citizens and metics vote in the Assembly, which governs Athens. Each year three of their number are chosen to be magistrates, called archons, and they lead the government. Themistocles is the most powerful archon this year.' She paused.

Nyresa swiftly glanced at Rhode to see where this history lesson was leading. Rhode's face was solemn, unreadable. Something fearful was coming.

'What I am about to tell you, Nyresa, must not be repeated. Many aristocratic Athenians have not been pleased with my uncle's reforms. They have resented the loss of power, especially in the courts and the Assembly. My uncle Cleisthenes is dead and I have heard the view expressed that it will take another generation for democracy to be truly secure in Athens. Our generation will either make or break my uncle's reforms. We live in precarious times. The forces of tyranny surround us, and one such tyrant – his name is Hippias – is very close indeed.'

'Hippias,' Nyresa repeated. She remembered what Glyka and Cherson had told her about him. 'He was the deposed dictator of Athens. Even though he's now old, Darius, wants to return him to power.' The memory of Cherson's murdered father and grandfather flashed across her mind.

Agariste nodded. 'If the Persians attack and conquer Athens, then Darius will reinstate him as dictator. Any survivors will be Hippias's slaves.'

'It won't happen!' Nyresa declared, bothered by Rhode's utter silence. 'The Athenians will never allow it to!'

'Nyresa, do you think the Athenians can defeat the Persians?' Nyresa was silent. 'What chance will Athens have if some of her people betray her and let the Persians in?'

Nyresa whispered: 'Who would do that? Why would anyone do that?'

No one spoke. The only sounds were of birds cracking seeds.

'My brother and my cousin are plotting to help Hippias re-enter Athens,' Agariste quietly declared. 'It is ironic that the Alcmaeonidae, who had exiled Hippias, should now be scheming for his return. Hippias has promised them power. All my uncle's reforms will be wiped out.

'This is what Rhode and I have been discussing, Nyresa. Now you know why we had to keep our talks secret. Treason is the highest crime of the state.' Agariste delivered her speech with elegant poise. Clearly, she had prepared her words carefully. 'Many aristocrats will not be sorry to see democracy annulled. So Athens will become a province of Persia. Darius will never give Hippias real power; and my brother and cousin will no doubt be betrayed by them both.'

'Why would they do this?' Nyresa whispered.

'Because they are foolish, Nyresa. Ambitious, vain and foolish. They do not think, they daydream. They're hungry for power.' Here her composure cracked. 'They don't realize that Hippias is just using them. And Darius will not stop at Athens. He will conquer the entire mainland – Thebes, Delphi, Eleusis – then go south to the Peloponnese, to conquer Sparta, Argos, Corinth, Epidaurus. Our men will be killed, our women transported across the empire into slavery. And my brother and cousin are helping to bring this disaster about.'

Nyresa covered her mouth with her hands. Agariste's voice was full of emotion, and Nyresa desperately wished she could help her.

Agariste calmed herself. She sat up straight, raised her chin, breathed slowly and dropped her shoulders. 'I have learned from powerful friends and from eavesdropping on my brother that the Persians will not strike this summer. For the next twelve to fourteen months their emperor is sending out calls for earth and water to the islands between Asia and Athens. And he is building hundreds of ships.'

She looked directly at Nyresa. 'Rhode has been my only confidante. We women can't fight wars but I think we can help thwart my brother's plot. I don't yet know exactly what he's planning but I will find out. Nyresa, your freedom to move about the city will help. You are young, foreign, not yet a parthenos, no one will suspect you.'

At that moment Tunnis entered the room with warm wine and sesame cakes. By her expression, Nyresa realized that she too had known Agariste's story of the Alcmaeonid treachery. Nyresa turned a mournful gaze on to Agariste and then to Rhode.

'Will you join us, Nyresa?' Agariste simply asked.

Thoughts of her friends, displaced and afraid because of war, flooded her mind. Then came thoughts of Thira, of her mother's grave and her favourite kore, of the view from the mountaintop, and the caldera's blue and yellow water. Suddenly she realized, with wonder, that she wasn't feeling afraid. Her fears, like her nightmares, had continued in Athens, but the more she learned of and faced real dangers, the less overwhelming imagined ones seemed.

'Yes, Agariste. I will.'

3. MIRON

Nyresa lay a bit late in bed the next morning, thinking. Agariste had said that the Persians would not attack until next summer – perhaps as long as a year and a half from now. Epiktiti had promised to collect Nyresa in a year, to take her home to Thira. As much as she wanted to go home, Nyresa was slowly realizing she did not want to abandon her friends. The statue of Athena battling the Giants on the portico of her ancient temple on the Acropolis came into her mind. She remembered the goddess's solemn, serene expression; her beautifully carved cape, with its border of twisting, intertwined snakes. I want to be like Athena, defending Athens, she thought.

After a few moments she threw back the covers with new determination. Today, finally, I will send Miron to Glyka, she thought. I have been away from Thira six months and do feel settled. I shall take him to the Pynx – the idea of Cherson darted through her mind – the highest point in the city. She dressed rapidly and, with Tunnis and Rhode's help, gathered Miron into his cage. She put into her bag the strip of flax, charcoal and twine needed to send the message.

As Nyresa strode along the path circling the Acropolis, she was delighted to hear a familiar voice.

'Every time we meet you're slinging some poor pigeon along, and yet you profess not to like them.' It was Cherson, laughing, enjoying teasing her.

She looked at him, embarrassed but secretly pleased.

'I *don't* like pigeons. If you notice, every time you see me I am *loosing* a pigeon! And anyway, "every time" means twice. It's just chance that I happen to be headed for the Pynx today to loose Miron. Good thing I didn't actually wait for you and your invitation.'

Cherson kept grinning. 'Well, I happen to be walking to the Pynx myself this morning. May I carry Miron's cage for you? Perhaps we'll run into Klio on the way.'

Nothing somehow seemed to be under Nyresa's control, she thought, not unhappily. She handed over the cage. She wouldn't worry about walking alone with a boy. After all, she wasn't yet a parthenos.

'We'll go up the Mousseion, the "hill dedicated to the muses", shall we?'

They ambled around the base of the Acropolis, passing the massive outcrop of marble on which trials were held, called the Areopagus. Cherson was busy telling Nyresa about the Areopagus and its trials, and she remembered what Agariste had said last night, about the resentment of the Athenian aristocracy at losing power to the courts and the Assembly.

'You're very quiet,' Cherson observed. 'What are you thinking about?'

'Nothing,' she lied, with a reassuring smile. Everything said last night was secret and, besides, she didn't want to think of it now.

Soon they came to the foot of a pine-covered hill. As they started on the wide path up the hill, Cherson took Nyresa's hand. The effect was electric. She stiffened and after a moment removed her hand. Neither said anything. They just kept climbing the hill.

She had been amazed by the feel of his hand. It was his strength that most surprised her. Her grandmother's hand never felt like this, or Glyka's, Rhode's, Thratta's or even Tunnis's.

Cherson was no less surprised. Nyresa's hand was not weak but delicate, soft, small. He glanced rapidly at her. It was, he saw, the right size to go with the rest of her, but how could anyone do anything with such a fragile hand? The thought of 'the rest of her' made his face burn with blushes.

She looked over at him, seeing his embarrassed face and the sinews of his strong neck. She looked around for something to talk about and saw, through the pine trees, a series of caves cut into the side of the hill. Their openings were wide so she could see quite far into them.

'What are those caves?' she asked.

'They say people have always lived in them,' he said, grateful for something to talk about. 'But these days they're empty, unless the criminal court, the Areopagus, imprisons a murderer there.'

This idea startled Nyresa into silence. The word Areopagus made her think again of treason and war. She forced herself to think of other things, and recalled Cherson's dreams of becoming a charioteer.

'Cherson, last autumn you told me you planned to win the quadriga. Is it at the Olympics that you wish to compete, as your ancestors did?' She looked up at him. He saw her dark eyes gleam through her lashes.

Without missing a beat, he answered, 'Yes. However, I also plan to win the quadriga at Delphi. And when I win this race,' he stole a quick look at her, 'I will have a bronze statue made of myself.'

She burst out laughing. Although she saw immediately that her laughter affronted him, she couldn't help it. 'A bronze statue? Life-size, I suppose?'

'Yes,' he replied deliberately. 'Standing in my chariot – the two-wheel sort, with a high front and four horses!'

'You're going to have a bronze statue made of you, with four horses, life-size . . .?'

'And an attendant on each side of the front pair.'

'So . . . you and two attendants and four horses and a chariot?'

'Yes.'

Just for a moment she wondered if he were mad. 'Cherson, no statues look like that,' she said slowly. 'Statues are carved or cast in single blocks. Gods or goddesses or men or women are inside their own block of stone or . . . or . . . space, somehow.'

'Mine will be different,' he said defiantly. 'I would want my face and body to seem real.'

'Would you have a welcoming smile, like a grave guard?'

'No. My face will be still, strong, determined.'

'You're pretty sure of yourself and your statue,' Nyresa teased. 'I'll have you know that my favourite kore on Thira doesn't smile either, and she was carved over a hundred years ago.'

'It isn't just that I want my statue to be solemn. I want it to be lifelike, as if that of someone you might know. Does your kore look like someone you know? Does she seem alive?' He really was asking her.

Nyresa thought for a few moments. 'No. What you are describing is different. My kore is a statue, after all.' The idea of a living statue unsettled her and she changed the subject slightly. 'If you win the quadriga, and prove yourself on the battlefield, and have a statue made in your honour, will your uncle take your name to the Assembly and ask them to confirm you a citizen and a member of his clan?'

Cherson nodded. 'Unless my uncle has already presented my name to the Assembly.'

'You *are* mad,' she cried, slapping his shoulder lightly, then running up the hill towards the wide marble plateau of the Pynx.

He bolted after her, delighted by her boldness.

They came immediately on to the plateau from the east side and saw vast, sweeping steps of white marble facing north. The place was empty now. Cherson playfully grabbed hold of Nyresa, swirling Miron's cage in the process.

'What did you say about my being mad?' he asked, frowning in mock menace.

She couldn't help but burst out laughing. Their eyes met. He leaned closer and kissed her. She felt wonderful, as though floating on a powerful wave. They both were grinning now and very pink, their eyes shining.

Suddenly Miron let out a furious screech. They looked over and saw him, miserable, in an upside-down cage. Nyresa never forgot the look he gave her. She and Cherson leaped over to the cage, truly apologetic. Cherson reached in to hold Miron, gently coaxing him from his cage. Meanwhile, Nyresa sat down on a step, pulling the flax and charcoal from one of the shopping baskets down at her side, and began composing her message to Glyka. There was room for only a few words – but so much to say! She thought hard and fast: ALL WELL IN ATHENS. MISS YOU. Cherson glanced down and read it. As he turned away to grab Miron's leg to be wrapped, she quickly added, on the reverse side: THERE'S A BOY. Confused by her own ridiculous message, but wanting more than anything for Cherson not to see it, she rapidly wrapped the flax around Miron's ankle and tied it securely with the string. Her eyes met Cherson's again when she took the bird from him. Then she walked towards the middle of the top marble sweep, to a specially carved platform with its own steps down to a lower level.

'You're standing on the bema,' Cherson called to her. 'That's where orators stand when they address the Assembly.'

She turned and gave Cherson a devastating smile.

'I shall release Miron on the bema!' she shouted. When she got to the centre of the bema, with a great whoosh of her arms, as she had done before with Agariste's bird, she threw his body up into the air. For a split second Miron seemed flustered, panicky. Then his strong wings began to beat and he pushed himself upwards on to a current of air – and was gone.

Nyresa and Cherson longingly followed his flight. As

Nyresa gazed, she could see the Acropolis in the background. For the first time she saw the full brilliance of the ancient temple of Athena. It dominated Athens, yet its excellence was subtle, simple, joining earth and sky, man and nature.

As the bird wheeled south, heading straight for Thira, Nyresa imagined its flight: across the plains of Attica and down to the last point on the peninsula, where the lovely temple at Sunium stands, a beacon for all sailors; then across the open Aegean, over the Cycladic Islands and finally down to Thira. In her mind's eye she saw Miron circling Thira, her Stronghili, the circular isle, her Kalliste, the fairest isle. She saw the deep blue crater in the centre of the steep, pink volcanic cliffs, forever covered by their mantle of white ash. Her hand felt again the bursting yellow bubbles in the middle of the caldera, and again she smelled the sulphurous sea. She watched Miron circle the temple to Apollo, overlooking the cliff, facing west, and heard again the singing of her grandmother. How long ago it was, how far away.

Cherson walked quietly up to her. He too had been strangely moved by the flight of the bird. Miron was gone and safe; what would happen to them? Just then a beautiful white pigeon flew into a pine tree above the marble plateau where they stood.

'Cherson! Have you ever seen such a bird? He is perfect,' she whispered. 'Is he natural? Is he a *bird*?'

Cherson smiled sadly. 'Yes, Nyresa, he is a bird, and not magical. He comes from . . . I don't know,' he shrugged his shoulders, 'from somewhere in the Persian empire.'

Nyresa whirled around, shocked. 'Is it an omen?'

'I don't know,' he admitted, 'but they say that when Mardonius's fleet foundered at Mount Athos, the white pigeons they were carrying flew off and came to the mainland. Mardonius brought these pigeons from Persia.'

Nyresa sighed and sat down on a marble bench carved into the hillside. Cherson sat beside her. Together they looked over Athens, at the houses, the Agora, the city walls, and the Acropolis. Beyond the city they saw the plains of Attica stretching to meet their encircling mountains. They saw the bright winter sky and the noonday sun.

Nyresa ran her fingers over her necklace and prayed silently to Artemis to protect her – and to protect Cherson, her grandmother, Rhode, Klio, Agariste and Tunnis.

'I heard a poem the other day,' Cherson said quietly. 'It is by Pindar. Have you heard of him?'

Nyresa shook her head.

'I memorized one verse because it is about winning races,' he admitted, shyly. 'Would you like to hear it?'

Nyresa smiled and nodded yes.

'. . . but blessed, worthy the poet's song, is the man
who by excellence of hand and speed in his feet
takes by strength and daring the highest of prizes –'

He turned a serious face to Nyresa. 'He also once wrote,
That which a man desires,
If he grasp, he must keep it in care beside him.
A year hence nothing is plain to see . . .'

Nyresa dropped her eyes. This was more of an outing

than she was prepared for. Out of shyness, embarrassment, excitement, nerves – suddenly Nyresa smiled up at Cherson. 'Come along, oh bronze charioteer. Let's go to the cobbler's shop to get warm. Klio says you often go there too.'

'That's fine, pigeon-lover,' he laughed, delighted with her teasing. Hand in hand, they walked back down the hill into Athens.

4. NEWS FROM AEGINA

From that momentous time in February when Nyresa promised to help Agariste and Rhode, and Cherson kissed her, her life in Athens had become extremely exciting, even though her daily routine hardly changed: long conversations with Rhode, shopping in the Agora for Tunnis, and gossiping at the cobbler's shop with Klio, Cherson and the cobbler. Often Gorgo sat with them, spinning and listening. Nyresa felt she had two lives: the Rhode–Agariste–Tunnis one, dependent upon messenger pigeon; and the Agora one, based in the cobbler's shop.

It was fun and frustrating 'talking' to Agariste through the birds. Very little could be written on the flax strips, but so far there had been little in the way of real news. Agariste had not been able to learn any more about the plans of her brother and cousin. The Persian emperor Darius had made clear that he would take his time preparing for war: every Greek city-state would receive the demand for earth and water; he would build a fleet of longships and transport ships. The first year of building was almost up and as the summer approached, there seemed to Agariste, Rhode and Nyresa no alternative but to wait. A whole year remained before the Persians were likely to attack. Surely Agariste's brother and cousin would slip up and reveal something of the enemy's plans.

Agariste visited Rhode and Nyresa about once every two months. On these visits they talked and talked, with Tunnis in the background, hovering protectively. Tunnis was a fearful soul, brave only in the defence of her beloved girls (for she now included Nyresa in her heart, as she did Rhode). Talk of treason terrified her and she did not mind in the least that the young ladies had nothing of significance to communicate.

The news from the Agora, though, was not good. Cherson had heard from sailors that Darius had ordered a Greek island near Cherson's homeland to hand over its ships to Persia. Klio received a scroll from her parents in Aegina where, according to rumour, there had already been skirmishes with Athenian forces. She sat beside Nyresa, at the Altar of the Twelve Gods, reading the scroll. The news so stunned her that she sat shivering with fear, indifferent to the sweet, late-spring weather.

'Oh Nyresa, I have learned such dreadful things,' she told her friend. 'There's been a civil war. The patriots won and took those who sided with the Athenians out of town to kill them. Seven hundred captives, Nyresa! One broke free and ran for sanctuary to the temple of Demeter, near our town, but the patriots caught up with him. When he wouldn't let go of the temple's door handles, they simply chopped off his hands – while his hands remained gripping the handles. Then they executed all seven hundred captives and, as they headed back to the city, the patriot executioners saw his severed hands still clutching the temple door handles.'

Nyresa felt ill and turned away from Klio.

'That's not all,' Klio continued in a distant voice. 'We are at war now with the Athenians. The only good news is that, miraculously, my father, my fiancé, and my future father-in-law were not involved, have not been killed. They wanted me to know; that's why they wrote.'

Slowly the precariousness of Klio's situation sank into Nyresa's consciousness: as an Aeginetan, she was an official enemy of Athens. Yet her removal to Athens by her parents meant there was no way she could return to Aegina. She could neither go forwards nor back.

'What am I to do, Nyresa?' Klio cried out.

Sympathy surged up in Nyresa's heart. 'You are surrounded by friends who love you, Klio. You have become a respected musician with many engagements at the symposia. Gorgo looks after you as a mother. This horror will come to an end, one day. Listen to me. One day the Greeks will live in peace, the threat of war with Persia, and of internal wars, will cease. One day you will return to Aegina, just as I will return to Thira.' Her eyes commanded Klio to believe her.

'You don't know that, do you?' Klio replied, her voice very low and solemn.

'No, I don't know, Klio. But it is what I believe, and we

must do all we can to make it happen. I will not be fearful and despairing. Nor should you be.'

The two girls looked at each other for a long moment. As one they rose and, arm in arm, left the Altar of the Twelve Gods to rejoin the world.

5. PANATHENAEA

Spring passed into summer. Klio heard nothing more from her parents. Nyresa heard nothing from Epiktiti; nor was there news of consequence from Agariste. The people of Athens tried not to think of their war with Aegina or of the coming war with Persia. The city was immersed in rehearsals, cooking and practising for its great festival, the Panathenaea. Athens would forget danger and rejoice in competitions: in poetry, music, athletics, horse and chariot races, boat races. Cherson made Nyresa laugh by telling how he was entering everything – the boxing, wrestling, sprint races. Everyone in Athens felt reassured to see preparations in full swing for the most important of Athens's festivals.

On the first day of the festival poetry and music were presented. Rhode was desperately jealous that Nyresa attended with Cherson. On the second day Nyresa saw Cherson compete in his many athletic events but not win. He told her firmly that this was because he was younger than most competitors in his category. On the third day it seemed that all five hundred thousand people in Athens, including Rhode with her porters, processed to the Acropolis in a massive parade.

They were led by the little girl-weavers, Gorgo's aristocratic pupils, proudly bearing Athena's specially woven cloak. At the end of the parade, the cloak would be draped over the wooden statue of Athena in the ancient temple on the Acropolis. Then came the sacrifice of the animals, the carcasses of which were carved into hunks of meat, distributed to all. Everywhere fires burned to cook the meat. Soon everyone in Athens was feasting on lamb and beef, bread and cake.

On day four Cherson had got permission to be a stable hand for the horses running in the chariot races and the horseback race. He was keenly aware that his uncle Miltiades would be around the horses, taking an interest. Here was a chance to make a good impression upon his important relative. Nyresa stood on the outside of the little corral that held the horses as they were prepared for their race. Then Miltiades entered the corral and came up to the horse Cherson was grooming. Nyresa stared at Miltiades, at his full but now greying beard and his thick hair. He had a strong face, attractive, but she couldn't tell if she thought he was kind or good.

Into the corral came two young gentlemen, apparently checking over their favourite horses. And right after them, from different sides of the corral, Themistocles and a comparably elegant, commanding, middle-aged man appeared. Nyresa recognized Themistocles from having seen him speak with the hetaera. Maybe the second man was also a politician or a magistrate.

She saw Miltiades turn to greet Themistocles and his

companion, and then glance, less warmly, at the two young Athenian aristocrats. He doesn't like those young men, she thought to herself. Themistocles and his companion also caught Miltiades's expression, following his eyes to the two youths. Nyresa saw the steady way each man took in the sight of the young gentlemen. They don't like the young ones, either, she thought. Who *are* those young men?

Then Miltiades brought Cherson into the conversation, much to Cherson's embarrassment. The three older men spoke generally of the Persian threat. Nyresa could overhear a lot of what they said because they spoke loudly, with the forced jollity of politicians. She could see the aristocratic youths in the corral eavesdropping too. She crept a little closer to try to hear more. Just then she heard Themistocles ask Cherson if he hoped to serve in the army.

Nyresa saw him burn with blushes as he answered. 'Thank you, sir. Yes, sir, I do hope to serve, to fight against the Persians.' Cherson's face was aflame for, as Nyresa knew, the one thing he wanted more than anything was to be allowed to go into military training. But only sons of Athenian citizens were allowed to join the army; his uncle would have to sponsor him. To sponsor him meant he would have to announce to the Assembly his paternity, that Miltiades's brother, Stesagoras, was Cherson's father. Nyresa watched Miltiades gazing at Cherson as though all this had nothing to do with him. Her heart sank. Then Miltiades spoke.

'Well, Cherson, it may be the Persians will arrive before traditional military training could be completed. But I could use a boy to shine my armour and keep my spear and sword sharpened. Would such training as a soldier appeal to you?' Miltiades's face still revealed no particular interest in the boy or his answer.

Cherson stared in disbelief. 'Yes, sir. Thank you, sir.'

'That settles it,' Themistocles said, laughing and then clapping Cherson on the shoulder. 'I'm glad to see one resident of Athens happy that the Persians are coming.' He was speaking very distinctly and loudly. What an odd thing to say, she thought. She didn't know what more to think.

Themistocles's companion, to her amazement, laughed confidently too, no less sure of the situation. 'Yes, indeed, Themistocles. There can't be many of those.' Both politicians laughed heartily as if, suddenly, the best of friends. Miltiades, turning out of the corral, continued chatting with the politicians as the three strolled away. The two young aristocrats, too, took the chance to leave.

Nyresa and Cherson exchanged warm, happy smiles. Then she waved goodbye and slid out through the crowd gathered around the corral, eager to communicate what she had just heard and seen to Rhode and Agariste.

She decided to circle the Acropolis on the Agora side, on her way home. As she passed through the top of the Agora, she was startled to see Klio and a servant in deep conversation. The servant looked familiar but Nyresa couldn't think why. They were sitting under some plane trees near the base of the Acropolis. Nyresa stopped and slunk slightly behind an olive tree. She was upset to see that Klio was crying and the servant was comforting her. Then the two women rose and moved out of sight. What did this mean? Why was Klio crying? Nyresa couldn't help feeling a little left out that Klio would talk to a servant if she were unhappy, not to her.

Nyresa arrived home, unsettled and unsure. She told Rhode all that had happened to her and they decided to contact Agariste, though Rhode thought she was still at the Agora watching the horse races.

Nor could they contact her on the fifth and last day of the festival, as Agariste was again at the competitions, this time for male strength and beauty and for the dance honouring Apollo's battle with the python at Delphi. Nyresa sneaked out alone in the evening to watch the nocturnal torch run, but did not see Agariste. While she was out, Rhode dispatched one of Agariste's pigeons. All Rhode felt safe in writing was: PLEASE VISIT SOON.

During the torch run Klio spotted Nyresa in the crowd. 'Nyresa!' Klio called, weaving her way through the crowd. 'Nyresa, I must talk to you.'

They turned into the lovely open-air building that held the elaborately carved fountain from which much of Athens got its water each day.

'Nyresa, you'll never believe what I have to tell you. You know how awful I felt after reading that scroll from my parents?' She looked earnestly into her friend's eyes.

Nyresa melted with pity. 'Yes, of course I remember,' she said gently.

'Yesterday I was upset again, and suddenly Melosa was beside me; the servant of that hetaera Gorgo warned us about. I've met her once or twice before, and she seemed worried about me. At first, of course, I wouldn't tell her

I was from Aegina, so I told her I was from an island and separated from my fiancé. But one thing led to another until she heard my whole story and I heard hers.'

'Klio! You told her you were from Aegina?' Nyresa cried, genuinely shocked.

'Oh, Nyresa, I said you'd never believe this! She and I have so much in common. She was married and lived in the city of Miletus, a Greek city on the Ionian coast. When civil war broke out in Miletus, her husband sided with the Persians and was killed. Melosa escaped by becoming the hetaera's servant and the two came to Athens together.'

Nyresa realized that the servant had looked familiar because she had seen her so many times in the fish queue with her beautiful mistress. 'Why didn't they move to some satrapy inside the Persian empire?' She couldn't think why Persian sympathizers would come to Athens.

'Because they're Greek! No Persian city would welcome them. So they decided to move to the most important of all Greek cities. When Melosa heard about the civil war on Aegina and that probably Aegina would give earth and water to Darius, she put her arm around me, saying that we both were victims of the wars between Persia and the Greeks.'

Nyresa was thinking fast. 'But Klio, she lost her husband, and he was fighting *for* the Persians. Your fiancé is no supporter of the Persians, is he?'

'He's for staying alive, Nyresa,' Klio answered steadily. 'He and his father say that anyone with money is welcome in their taverna, be he an Aeginetan, Spartan, Corinthian,

Athenian, or even a Persian. He and his family have no wish to side with anybody. Nor, for that matter, does my family.'

Nyresa looked back at her friend, thinking these things were less simple than she had thought. 'I'm glad you have found a friend in Melosa, Klio. I'm sorry for what has happened to her, and I hope a better future awaits you.' To her surprise, Nyresa felt a tear trickle down her cheek.

Klio threw her arms around her. 'Oh, Nyresa, what a time we all are having,' she whispered, and then darted away into the darkness to rejoin Gorgo.

Agariste, Rhode and Nyresa were finally able to meet the day after the festival. Nyresa told Agariste about the young aristocrats at the corral. She described them as they looked over the horses. She gave an account of the exchange between Cherson and Miltiades, and how Themistocles and the other middle-aged man had behaved. She told her how Miltiades had appointed Cherson to be his armour-bearer and serve in the army on the battlefield. Lastly she told them about Klio and Melosa. At one point Agariste interrupted her to say that the companion of Themistocles was very probably Aristides, his rival. They were the two most powerful politicians in all Athens.

Otherwise, Agariste listened intently. When Nyresa had finished, Agariste sat in silence, thinking. The other two waited patiently. Finally Agariste spoke.

'Nyresa, tell me what the young aristocrats looked like.' Her cold expression alarmed Nyresa.

'I could only see one's face clearly. I suppose he had

regular features which one might call handsome, but he looked hungry, eager. He flashed his teeth when he smiled and darted his eyes around, as though searching for prey.' She looked back at Agariste.

'The man you saw was Megacles, my brother. And his friend in the corral was my cousin.' Agariste stared into the middle distance. She spoke slowly. 'Do you see what this means?'

The two looked blankly at her.

'We now know that the rulers of Athens suspect my brother of treason, and we have a way to discover how Hippias is communicating with his Athenian allies.'

'How?' Nyresa burst out.

'Through Klio, Nyresa. She is the perfect link: my brother's symposia, the hetaera's dinners, Melosa. Although she and I have not been introduced, I am sure I have seen her. Is she not extraordinarily pretty?' Nyresa nodded. 'She has often come to my family's house to play at the symposia of my brother and cousin. At the very least, Klio can tell us if the men let slip any word about a plot. Perhaps the hetaera attends these symposia, and perhaps my brother and cousin attend her dinners? Klio might be asked to play there too. And Melosa would know of any pro-Persian collaborators in Athens, because of her employer's sympathies.'

'But can we expect Klio to help us – much less Melosa?' Rhode asked.

Agariste looked at Nyresa, who now was deep in thought. 'Can we expect Klio to help, Nyresa?'

'Yes, I'm sure she will. And she'll be able to tell us more about Melosa.'

Rhode leaned back in her chair. 'How strange to think that your sad Aeginetan flute player is our link to the Persian emperor. That, thanks to her, we can find out what is discussed at the symposia. Through her we may learn details of the plot and who is involved. We may discover how the plotters communicate with Hippias. We already know Hippias speaks with the emperor.'

'Yes, it's true,' Agariste chimed in. 'She can find Melosa in the fish queue and arrange to play at her mistress's dinners and at my brother's symposia. Then she can tell you whatever she learns.'

Nyresa recalled Gorgo's strange words to Klio many weeks ago at the cobbler's shop: 'You will be crucial in these matters, my dearest girl, because of your gentleness and loving heart. You will do what no one else can do.'

6. CHOICES

A chill was in the air. The festival was over and autumn about to begin. Nyresa had been feeling unsettled lately, as though her mood were changing with the seasons. The decision to involve Klio in the conspiracy worried her. Klio had too much on her mind; every day she waited in dread for news from Aegina. Now Nyresa was to ask her to combine the duties of a spy with those of a musician who lived off her fees. And she would be spying in the service of Athens – the enemy of Aegina.

But something else worried Nyresa. Yesterday her uncle informed her he'd received a message from Epiktiti that she would have to be away another year on her pilgrimage. And last night Nyresa had had a terrific nightmare, worse than any since she had arrived in Athens a year ago. In it she saw a field littered with dead soldiers, flies licking their eyes, the summer sun heating their bloated corpses. Across the battlefield, for so she supposed it was, she saw Cherson calling to her. She started to run to him when suddenly the earth began shaking. Rocks tumbled down upon the plain. Stones bounced on the trembling earth. The rest of the dream was all too familiar. The earth's crust closed up on her and all was silent. She cried out but no one rescued her. Only when Rhode and Tunnis appeared over her, gently calling to her and stroking her hair, did she awake.

A creeping fear seemed to fill her thoughts – not just when she remembered that the Persians were preparing to attack next summer. Cherson was the one shining star in her life, but even liking him seemed dangerous. She did not have her grandmother's approval, and had not mentioned him to her aunt and uncle in case they disapproved or took away her freedom. By now, aged thirteen, she should be a parthenos. She sighed. Next summer, she thought, all will be known: grandmother will return and meet Cherson, I will become a parthenos, and the Persians will attack.

In such a mood, Nyresa hurried among the fallen leaves of the plane trees to the cobbler's shop to meet Klio.

Once in the cobbler's shop the two girls took their stools deep into the corner, under the window behind a tall shelf of shoes. Gorgo sat in the opposite corner, spinning. Nyresa was quiet and kept her face turned away from Klio, which puzzled her. Klio watched the cobbler light his brazier for the first time this season and was reassured by the familiar crackling and tumbling of the coals.

Klio, aware of this heaviness about Nyresa, was about to inquire when Nyresa surprised her by saying, 'Cobbler, please, I have a very important favour to ask of you. Would you shut the shop for a few minutes? I have a great deal to tell you all and decisions must be made.'

Gorgo nodded solemnly. When the cobbler had closed up the shop, the two girls and the two adults sat around the brazier while Nyresa told them everything. She ended by saying, 'So, Klio, will you help? Will you speak with Melosa to see if she will help?'

The cobbler wore a worried expression. He is frightened for Klio, Nyresa thought. Maybe he's right . . . Gorgo's face was impassive but intent. 'Do *you* think Klio should do this, Gorgo?' Nyresa asked. 'Do you?'

Gorgo still said nothing, but turned her face towards Klio, receptive to Klio's reactions and thoughts. Gorgo then turned towards the brazier.

Nyresa could tell it was settled, but how?

'Yes, Nyresa,' Klio responded. 'I will help. I expect the Persians to attack Athens. They may spare Aegina or they may not. But here the men will die and the women be enslaved and deported across the Persian empire. They will kill Gorgo and Rhode, the old and the lame. They will send you and me, Nyresa, to a province hundreds of miles east of here, where we will be forced to bear some farmers' children and work their farms for the rest of our lives. You were right, Nyresa. We must resist, regardless of the odds. So, yes, I will help. I will speak with Melosa.'

Gorgo nodded. The cobbler sank into greater gloom. Nyresa felt chilled.

'Come then,' Nyresa said fiercely. 'Come with me to Rhode's house. She can send a message to Agariste. Perhaps Agariste will be able to "visit the lame" today and we can tell her and Rhode everything.'

7. THE PATRON

Klio pressed herself into the dark doorway of an empty house, trying to hide. Her face, she knew, was pink and puffy from crying. She looked up into the cold autumn night and watched the clouds scud past the moon. She fought for self-control.

The evening had been precisely what she and her friends, old and new, had been waiting for: a symposium at the home of Agariste's brother Megacles. Finally, nearly a month after Nyresa had enlisted Klio's help, Megacles had hired her to play. By then Klio had met Agariste and Rhode, and understood what they needed to know. This evening had begun reasonably and in good humour, with six young men enjoying each other's company. Excellent fish was served: a sea perch. Each youth ate bread with his fish and drank wine, politely and considerately. They reclined on the couches, slaves having removed their sandals. They ate cheese, onions, figs and garlic with their bread and fish. As the meal progressed, the professional musicians, including Klio and the other flute girls, had to be careful that the drinkers did not mistake them for dancing girls, bad girls. Klio noticed that the host had spent a great deal of money on the evening. The sea perch was especially expensive, as was the quality and quantity of wine drunk. The host had even hired a poet to recite verses while playing the lyre.

But when the dishes were cleared away and the guests had washed their hands, and the host, the lord of the feast, began mixing the wine with water, Klio grew worried. The drinking cups he brought out were unusual; they held twice the amount of wine as the shallow, saucer-like kylix most households used. Worse still, the host added hardly any water, nothing like the traditional mixture of five parts water to two parts wine. The uncut drink went straight to the men's heads and soon they were shouting and arguing and pawing at the female entertainers. They were drinking in the Scythian fashion – of wine uncut with water, Klio realized with alarm.

This was not what a symposium was supposed to be like. A symposium was supposed to be an occasion of rational discussion – of politics, poetry, metaphysics. The wine was meant to enliven the conversation. The words spoken and the wine drunk were to complement each other. There were rules to a well-run symposium: a libation was offered to Dionysus, a hymn sung in his praise, then the lord of the feast was elected. Each guest in turn made a little speech.

133

Discussion or discourse was meant to be the centre of the evening, not drinking. The importance of the conversation and the small draughts served kept the effects of the drink under control.

That evening, amid the shouting and the anger and the crude remarks, Klio heard something that shocked her, something she was sure she was not meant to hear. Megacles boasted he had spent last evening with Athens's most beautiful hetaera. With suddenly sobered faces, the other guests nodded. Megacles then walked around the couches of the dining room until he came to the couch of one large, red-faced man, placed a hand on the red-faced man's shoulder, and said, 'We are honoured this evening to have with us her friend, the merchant from Aegina.' Respectful murmurings came from the other guests. Slowly, with great ceremony, he continued, 'To us, he brings greetings from our most important and serious patron.' Here the host looked solemnly round the room. 'To the patron!' He held up his drinking cup.

'To the patron!' all the intoxicated men shouted.

Klio played on as the host spoke, her eyes lowered. The toast rang in her ears, primed as she was for any hint of conspiracy. When she finished playing and opened her eyes, Megacles was smiling at her, flashing his teeth, his eyes locked on to her face. She could almost read his mind: Have you been listening? Are you a spy? Klio gathered her things, bowed, and left the room.

She hoped he would not follow her and question her about what she'd heard. She vowed she would never go to Megacles's house again – it was too dangerous and the behaviour of the men at the symposium had frightened her.

Later that night she told Gorgo what she had seen and heard. Gorgo listened carefully. 'You must tell Nyresa and Rhode and Agariste,' Gorgo declared. Klio nodded.

8. BEADS

Agariste listened intently. 'A merchant from Aegina? That is the collaborators' connection with Hippias?'

Klio nodded. She spoke quietly. 'Because Aegina is sympathetic with the Persians, it is easy for a merchant to travel between the Ionian coast and Aegina. And even though Athens is at war with Aegina, it seems trade goes on as usual. So the merchant delivers messages between your brother and the hetaera – and Hippias and the emperor.'

'But you discovered it, Klio. Now we know the chain of command, from my brother and the hetaera right through to the emperor himself. Our next move is to discover their plot and then foil it. We need Melosa's help. She can make sure that Klio is hired for dinners or symposia when the merchant visits. She will also know her mistress's mind and may herself discover something of the traitors' plans.' Here Agariste flushed, embarrassed and upset to find herself referring so matter-of-factly to her brother and cousin as traitors.

Rhode filled the silence. 'Klio, do you think Melosa will join us?'

Klio was silent for a few moments. 'I don't know. We've had several long talks over the past weeks. She blames the Athenians for supporting the Ionian Revolt in which her husband died. Yet I feel she is a good person. Before her husband died she was probably happy and looking forward one day to being a mother. If she could be reminded of those early days perhaps her heart might soften. We met because she took pity on my tears.'

The four looked at each other and then down, thinking. Tunnis, ever in the background, poured each a cool drink of wine mixed with cold water.

'We probably have nine to twelve months before the Persians attack,' Agariste said. 'In that time, you or perhaps Nyresa must reach Melosa. She has access to the hetaera and to the merchant. Klio, try to stay close to her and learn – from her and the symposia – what you can.'

Nyresa lifted her head to speak and addressed the others. 'I would like your permission to tell Cherson about all this. He is very important to me now and I wish to keep nothing from him.'

Each young woman reacted similarly. Their eyes smiled in sympathy while their mouths expressed dismay. Agariste took the lead. 'You know how serious this is. The honour of my family, the fate of Cleisthenes's reforms, of Athens itself and of all the Greek people, hangs on the coming war with Persia. We must do everything we can to thwart my brother's plot. If you trust Cherson to help us, then you have my permission to tell him.'

Nyresa looked into the face of each of her friends, then nodded. Their counter-conspiracy was growing.

Two weeks later, while shopping for Tunnis in the Agora, Nyresa caught sight of Melosa in the fish queue. I must try to speak with her, she thought. As she approached, she heard the fishmonger joking. 'Come now, Melosa. This is the end of October. Where am I going to find a gilt head? Even in season, they're the rarest of fish.'

Melosa shrugged. 'That's what my mistress says she wants.'

'Be reasonable, Melosa. I can't sell what I haven't got. Wouldn't she settle for conger eel? Or sea perch, grey mullet, red mullet?'

'Then give me the biggest grey mullet you have. And if you get something better tomorrow, save it for me.'

Nyresa had been studying Melosa's face. Klio was right; the face did reflect a hardened and unhappy heart. Still, Melosa had taken pity on Klio and had reached out to comfort her. Nyresa would try. Just as Melosa turned to leave the queue, having received her mullet and swaddled it like a baby, Nyresa approached her but suddenly gave out a little cry. Everyone looked up and Melosa stepped back in alarmed surprise. 'What is it?' she asked.

How could Nyresa answer? In that second, standing before Melosa, she'd seen ten pastel beads exactly like her own, around Melosa's neck. But Melosa came from Miletus, didn't she? The necklace made her think of her dead mother and her grandmother. Was Melosa like them – a woman of Thira?

As she stood there, she realized Melosa was staring back at her beads. Nyresa tried to read her expression, but could not. The two locked eyes for a moment, then Melosa turned quickly away and was soon out of sight.

V

Demeter would not lift her curse. Zeus was wild with anger, and distraught. Like Persephone, he could not undo what had been done. He flew to his mother, the goddess Rhea, who loved her children, Zeus, Demeter and Hades.

Rhea was expecting him. She listened to his story and suggested a compromise: Persephone would spend four months a year with Hades, as Queen of the Underworld, and the remaining eight months on earth with Demeter. That way, when Persephone returned to earth, her arrival would revive all living things. The tender light green leaves would again appear on the trees. Plants would sprout, fruit trees blossom, and mothers would again be with child. Only when she returned to Hades would the earth fall barren, cold and dark. For four months the earth would be dead, while Demeter mourned the loss of her daughter. When mother and daughter embraced again, it would revive. The earth would bloom in spring.

CONSPIRACY

490 BC

1. EARTH AND WATER

All winter, rumours of war swirled like the snow. Athens was at war with Aegina, and everyone was afraid Aegina would grant Darius earth and water. Such an alliance would be disastrous, for it would give Darius a foothold right across the bay from Athens. From Aegina, he could easily send his navy and army to destroy the city. War was coming; the sides were forming.

It seemed that the more war was rumoured, the less frequently Agariste's brother and cousin convened symposia with their friends. Klio had been hired only once all winter, and nothing of import had been discussed. Melosa still came regularly to the fish stall, but kept to herself, head down. Agariste, Rhode, Nyresa and Klio could only wait, hearing constant reports of Darius's military preparations. The cobbler, Gorgo and Tunnis were a comfort – they understood the young women's fears. Nyresa had told Cherson about the plot, but he was worried Agariste's suspicions were based more on rumour than fact. It worried him too that Nyresa and Klio were trying to compile evidence for treason against one of Athens's most powerful families. If caught and challenged, what would they say? Who would believe two foreign girls, especially one from Aegina? They would be in great danger.

One afternoon, as winter turned to spring, Nyresa sat in the cobbler's shop talking quietly with Klio. Cherson came running into the shop, alarmed but excited.

'Darius's messengers have arrived! They came to Athens this morning demanding earth and water. Miltiades and the other commanders hurled the messengers into the Pit where criminals are executed, telling them that they could fetch their own earth and water.'

Nyresa's response mirrored Cherson's worried look. Klio and the cobbler sat, stunned. Not a sound was heard as he continued. 'And there's more. Aegina has offered Darius earth and water. It has joined with Persia against us.'

'What will happen now?' said Nyresa.

'The rumour is that Darius has appointed a new commander called Datis. "Leader of the Hosts" he's called. Mardonius has been set aside.' Cherson glanced over at Nyresa and Klio and then at the cobbler. 'Datis has gathered infantry, cavalry and naval forces at a port south of Persia, on the Mediterranean.' He shrugged his shoulders. 'There are wild rumours about the size of the force: from eighty to three hundred thousand.'

'How many Athenian soldiers are there?' Klio asked.

'Miltiades hasn't briefed me yet,' Cherson said with a short laugh. 'I don't know how many the Persians really are, but it'll be fewer than rumoured – you must not take every rumour seriously. In the Agora they say Miltiades is petitioning the Assembly to free a number of slaves to bring our army up to full strength. And men over fifty are being called up. We might have as many as nine thousand men.'

The girls now looked at the cobbler, who sat staring out of his window. He was over fifty. 'Here comes Melosa,' he alerted them. 'Perhaps her mistress is expecting the merchant again ... Then again he might be having difficulty entering Athens, now that Aegina has given earth and water.'

Klio immediately walked out of the shop, over to the fish queue, and spoke to Melosa. Cherson, Nyresa and the cobbler watched through the window.

After a few minutes of what looked like animated and friendly talk, Klio returned. 'Good news at last. Melosa's mistress is planning a series of elegant dinner parties and Melosa has asked me to play at them.'

Nyresa sat brooding. She remembered what the cobbler had once told her: 'The people in that queue run this city or will determine its fate. Mark them well, young miss ... Who is plotting? Consider where these people get the money for their expensive delicacies. Oh, yes, the fish stall is an excellent place for discovering secrets ... Who knows what ideals these people have betrayed in their greed!'

The hetaera is greedy, Nyresa thought, and Melosa is vengeful.

2. 'ALL HAS BEEN AGREED'

Rhode hated more than ever being confined. Her mother was constantly occupied purchasing beautiful objects for the house or lovely new material for her himations and tunics, while her father, though always jovial and pleasant with Rhode, rushed off each day to the Agora or Phaleron, keeping track of his merchant ships. The occasional visits of Agariste were a huge relief to her. Sometimes Agariste brought her son, now seven years old, and he played contentedly with Rhode's pigeons. Agariste too had been restive, confined to the women's part of her own house. At least she could visit Rhode from time to time. Agariste had not heard the rumours from the Agora, but she did bring valuable gossip from the Alcmaeonid house where her extended family lived in various wings. Servants and slaves who waited upon Agariste's brother told her where he was going and what his mood was. Sometimes their cousin visited Megacles, and she heard about that too.

Today, Agariste told Rhode and Nyresa what Klio had anticipated: Agariste's brother and cousin were invited, in a few weeks' time, to the hetaera's for a special evening. The dinner was to be both extremely lavish and very private. The same information had come from the Agora, through Klio and Melosa. The circle was complete.

The day of the hetaera's dinner, Cherson and Nyresa were walking along the base of the Mousseion when the

Assembly meeting on the Pynx concluded and the men came streaming down the hill. They were all talking excitedly. Cherson and Nyresa eavesdropped.

The Assembly, this bright, cool spring day, had been called to announce the latest news to the fearful city. The Persian fleet, under the commander Datis, had set sail for Athens. But at its first port of call, a Greek island where the Persians expected victory, they had dramatically lost, thanks to a freak thunderstorm that saved the outnumbered inhabitants. Everyone credited the goddess Athena with bringing the storm. Now the Persian fleet had set sail again, but whether they travelled north or west, the Athenian men did not know. Nor did they know which direction was better for Athens.

Just then Cherson nudged Nyresa, gesturing towards two impressive figures walking several paces ahead of them. One, Nyresa recognized, was Miltiades, the commander of the Athenian forces and blood uncle to Cherson. The other she didn't know, but Cherson told her about him. His name was Kallimachos and he was one of the top magistrates or archons of Athens, along with Themistocles.

'Because he is an archon,' Cherson told her, 'he outranks Miltiades. Kallimachos is known as the "Polemarch". Officially the Polemarch leads the army and will make offerings to the gods on behalf of the army. Kallimachos is an amazing man. He will compete in the games of the Panathenaea – and he'll have a good chance of winning in spite of his being so old.'

Cherson clearly was impressed by the Polemarch, so

Nyresa studied him carefully. She watched the citizens descend the hill. These men governed Athens, she thought. They were also its artists, playwrights, aristocrats, shopkeepers and farmers. And they were its soldiers. They were Cherson's world, she reflected. Old and young, fair haired and dark, scrawny and fat, Athens's citizenry jostled along as it descended the hill, to merge again with the city.

On the appointed evening, Klio went to the hetaera's house, wearing her most attractive but simple tunic. It was near the beginning of June and already quite warm. She entered an elegant room filled with couches and pillows. Reclining on the central couch was a stunning beauty. Klio had heard that the hetaera did as she pleased, voiced her opinions, and was respected for her wisdom and skill in politics. She was known for priding herself on winning the hearts of powerful men so she could influence their minds and affect their decisions. This much was common knowledge – but Klio, knowing all that she did, felt nervous standing before this woman.

During the dinner Klio had played beautifully, forcing herself to concentrate on the rhythm and feeling of the music. She was so at one with the music that the men gazed at her as though she were a muse or divinity. Even the coarsest of the diners paid homage to Klio that evening.

Then, at last, Klio overheard something significant. At one interval between pieces, Agariste's brother turned to his friends and said, quite distinctly, 'All has been agreed. The signal too.' The others nodded.

146

Klio pretended not to have heard, but she remembered every word. After what seemed like an age, her part in the dinner was over and she quickly slipped out.

The next day Agariste went to Rhode and Nyresa's house to meet with Klio and hear what she had learned. On the way her servant told her of the latest news from the Agora: Datis had sailed west, not north. The Persian fleet was attacking islands in its path, burning temples and houses, slaughtering and enslaving the people. They were heading towards Athens.

'There are a great many islands between the Ionian coast and Athens,' Agariste replied evenly. 'I shouldn't worry yet. I believe we have at least three months before they arrive.'

Klio told what she had overheard: 'All has been agreed. The signal too.'

'Was the merchant from Aegina at the dinner?' Agariste asked.

Klio shook her head: no.

'But the cobbler said he has been to his shop recently,' Nyresa told Agariste.

Klio studied Agariste's face. 'Agariste, will you speak now to your brother, to dissuade him from carrying out this plot?'

'No, Klio. He would never listen to me. As my husband is away, Megacles is head of household. All that would happen is that I would be sent out of the city – for my own "safety". Our circle would be broken; it would be even harder to prevent or foil his plot. And I can't tell anyone else what we have learned. For the sake of my family's

147

honour I hope we can foil my brother's plot without exposing his treachery. I will try to hide his involvement if possible. But first and foremost we must save Athens.'

3. SAVED

That summer, tensions in Athens were high. The Agora, usually full of gossip and rumour, was quiet. People did not speak of Datis, the Persians or war. The Persians sailed from island to island. Linked arm in arm, the Persian soldiers formed themselves into a human chain across the entire width of an island and then walked across it, hunting down enemies. No one escaped. The Persians picked the best-looking boys and castrated them, turning them into eunuchs to serve in the royal court. The most beautiful girls were sent directly to the emperor at Susa, to serve as slaves. The rest of the population was enslaved and their settlements, sanctuaries and temples burnt to the ground. As they came closer to Attica, the Persians took the islanders' children as hostages and destroyed the farmland.

The people of Athens let the preparations for this coming summer's Panathenaea completely absorb them. The olive-wood statue of Athena, with the cloak woven by the little girls, had been carried with great ceremony down to the sea at Phaleron and washed. The first day of the festival had come once again, with the swearing-in ceremony for the judges and contestants. Nyresa watched with pride as Cherson was sworn in to compete in the races the next day. Now that he was nineteen he had a better chance. He had been practising his sprinting and hoped to place, if not to win.

Nyresa watched as he exercised and prepared for competition. She saw his uncle Miltiades talking quietly with him, then clap him on the back as if wishing him well. Cherson looked deathly worried. Unable to speak to him until after the race tomorrow, Nyresa headed home, anxiety filling her pretty face.

She ran into a group of drunken aristocrats as she wended her way along the narrow streets to her house. They were singing and laughing.

The loudest was shouting: 'Sythifisian drinking . . . n-no . . . Scytifinian drinking . . . We've been Scythiathusian drinking.' He howled to his friends. 'What is it? What have we been doing?' The others tried to say the phrase but gave up in peels of inebriated laughter. Then they saw Nyresa and surrounded her.

'You're far too pretty to be walking alone, my girl,' one man admonished her playfully.

'Far, far too pretty,' his companion agreed, and reached out to her long black curls to lift and drop them.

'As charming a little figure as you have and not yet a parthenos?' the loudest mocked. 'Why, how old are you? You must be fourteen if you're a day. I think I shall marry you, pretty little girl. Perhaps right now, right here! What do you say, my friends? Will you act as witnesses to this marriage?' Others cheered him on.

Nyresa at first blushed, then began to feel afraid. Maybe she was too old to walk the streets alone.

Suddenly a woman's harsh voice cut through the uproar, scattering the revellers. 'Stand back, you vermin! Stand back or I'll whip you to your senses. Back, I tell you.'

The gentlemen and Nyresa looked around to see fury on the face of a middle-aged woman. It was Melosa!

The men quickly dispersed. As they staggered away from the outraged Melosa, the loudest called back, 'Get away, you old skank. Crone. Pig's bladder!'

Nyresa was too scared to speak. Melosa ran to her. She took hold of both her shoulders and asked anxiously, 'Are you all right? Did they hurt you?'

Nyresa shook her head: no. Sobs burst out of her, shaking her body and filling the air. People's heads appeared at windows but Melosa waved them away. Little by little Nyresa calmed down, while Melosa hugged and rocked her, the two standing entwined in the street.

Nyresa fought to regain control. 'Thank you, Melosa. Oh, that was awful.'

'The men were very drunk. Forget them. But you are too old now, young lady, to walk alone.' After a pause she asked gently, 'Tell me, how did you know my name?'

'You saved me!' Nyresa smiled through tear-stained, tangled hair, still too upset to be on her guard. 'I knew your name from Klio, my good friend. She has told me all about you. She said you came from Miletus. But . . . but then I saw your beads that day in the fish queue. Are you Thiran?'

Melosa smiled sadly. 'I was born and grew up in Thira, though my husband came from Miletus, where we lived. Yes, I remember our meeting at the fish queue.' She gave a little laugh. 'I was as upset as you. No one had recognized my beads before. And when I saw the same sort around your neck I knew you knew.'

Nyresa looked deeply into Melosa's eyes. 'Don't you miss Thira? I miss it every day.' She appealed to Melosa in a burst of confiding. 'I so loved to sit on the mountaintop, right in front of the platform where the boys dance. Do you know where I mean?'

Melosa's face creased into smiles and she nodded.

'I used to swing my feet and scuff my sandals on the cliffside while I stared for hours at the criss-crossing boats and wheeling birds.' Memory flooded Nyresa's mind. 'And my friend Glyka and I ran down the mountain, on that goat path, and we used to swim in the sea, by the beautiful wind-sculpted ash cliffs, and sail all around the island and into the caldera. It seems like so long ago. Don't you miss it?' Sobs were beginning again to form in her chest.

'I do, Nyresa. I do,' Melosa whispered. Nyresa was too wrapped up in her memories to notice that Melosa knew her name.

'My favourite, though, my favourite thing to do was to sit in the graveyard, on that northern slope, surrounded by the tall, sweet grave guardians, at . . .'

'At your mother's grave . . .' Melosa chimed in.

'Yes, at her grave, beside my kore, the one who doesn't smile. Do you know that one, too?' Nyresa looked up hopefully. Then a shadow crossed her face. She frowned, and fear crept in. 'Melosa, how did you know my mother's grave? How did you know my name?' Her eyes now were large.

'Don't be afraid, Nyresa. After we saw each other's necklaces, I made a point of finding out who you were. You have so many friends in the Agora that it was not difficult.' She laughed then she grew serious again. 'Yes, I knew your mother. We are the same age. I went to her wedding and I attended her funeral, Nyresa. I remember seeing you as a newborn. Soon after that I left Thira. The rest Klio has probably told you.'

Nyresa stood still and looked in silence at Melosa. Then she took a deep breath. 'If you love Thira too, how could you help Persia? How can you help those who would enslave and deport Klio?' Melosa paled as Nyresa looked at her. 'And they will kill my gentle cousin Rhode, who is crippled, and Klio's kind guardian, Gorgo, who is old and blind. And all the men I know will be killed. My uncle, the cobbler . . .'

Now Melosa looked away. The only sound was of the fourteen-year-old's uneven, shuddering sighs. 'What will happen here in Athens,' Melosa answered quietly, 'happens all over our world, all the time. Some people survive, some don't.' There was a distant note in her voice.

'But you have saved *me*. Why did you do that? You didn't have to. Girls are attacked all the time, but you saved me.'

Nyresa's eyes sought Melosa's. Melosa leaned against the wall, one arm across her waist, her other hand over her mouth. 'I saved you because I knew you, I knew your mother, your father and your grandmother. I saved you because what the men were doing was wrong.'

152

'Is it not wrong for Persians to attack Athens?' Nyresa swayed, weakened by so many intense emotions. Melosa stepped forwards to steady her, then stepped back again. Nyresa's face darkened. 'My friend the cobbler calls some people the "fish eaters", the opsophagos. He says they indulge their appetites and that their appetites dominate their minds and hearts. You work for a fish eater, Melosa. She sends you to buy fish all the time, while she plots against Athens and its government. She is greedy.' She stared at Melosa, whose face was turned from her. 'Are you a fish eater, Melosa?'

A smile forced itself across Melosa's face. 'Am I an opsophagos? That's the strangest thing anyone ever asked me.' She laughed a little. 'Well, I *do* like fish. And I do like tasty food with my bread. All that's "opson", so in that sense, yes, I am an opsophagos. But . . . do I let my appetite dominate my mind and heart? No. I don't think so, Nyresa.'

'But how can you work for your mistress?' Nyresa asked. 'Please . . . explain.'

Melosa gave her a long look. 'Shall we walk as we talk?' she asked, and Nyresa nodded. 'This has been a strange time for me,' Melosa said. 'When I first came to Athens nine years ago I was furious. My husband had been killed in war and I blamed Athens. Athens gave me a safe berth but I felt alone – and in my anger I still wanted Persia to triumph over the Athenians.' Melosa turned her head to look at Nyresa, then smiled gently. 'Time has calmed me down, though I still have a temper! But seeing you has reminded me of my Thiran past. And Klio's story has shown me that one cannot control one's fate or resent it. We are all subject to the whims of the gods.' She glanced sadly now at Nyresa. 'I work for my mistress because her job gives me a home, food, "opson",' she said.

Nyresa was thinking hard. 'We are subject to the whims of the gods, but sometimes we can show the gods' will through our actions,' she said. 'We can *choose* to act in good ways, like you chose to save me just now.' She took a deep breath. 'Melosa, help us. Help us foil the plot of your mistress and of the Alcmaeonidae.'

Melosa's eyes opened wide. 'You know of this? Klio knows too?' She stepped back and leaned against the wall. Nyresa nodded. Melosa sighed. Neither spoke. Then, slowly, Melosa raised her hand and patted each bead in her necklace. She gave Nyresa a long, keen look. She smiled and stood straight.

'I *will* help you,' she replied. 'And I will help Klio.' She turned a brilliant smile now on Nyresa. 'I will again be proud of being Thiran and Greek. You're right, my mistress *is* an opsophagos. And two men of the Alcmaeonidae clan have decided to join with her to help Hippias retake Athens. Hippias says he will share the governing of Athens with them. He promises to marry my mistress and to give her all the respectability and power she has ever craved.'

'But what exactly is the plot?' Nyresa urged.

Melosa sat down on the stone kerb of the packed-earth street, and Nyresa sat beside her. 'When they land, the Persian commander will split his force. He'll send half with the cavalry on ships to disembark further down the coast and march to Athens. If the Spartans arrive to help Athens, making that disembarkation unsafe, the Alcmaeonidae will alert the Persian ships. A shield, hidden in the coastal hills, will be held up and flashed to the Persian ships, warning them not to land.'

Nyresa hadn't moved a muscle as she listened. 'Where do those ships go then, if the shield is flashed?'

'They turn away from the shore and sail the long route to Athens, which will take them thirty-six hours. By then, they expect their comrades on shore to have won the initial battle and marched on to take Athens.'

'Is it likely the Spartans will arrive in time?' Nyresa asked.

'No,' Melosa answered grimly. 'The Persian command has timed the battle to take place in the middle of a Spartan holy festival, knowing the Spartans will not come until their festival is over. The Persian commanders figure they can count on six days between landing on the beach at Marathon – where Hippias has advised them to engage the Athenians – and the Spartans arriving.'

After a brief pause Nyresa said, very calmly, 'If the shield were held up, even though no Spartans had arrived, the Persians would turn away and take the long route to Athens by sea?'

'Yes,' Melosa agreed, unsure of Nyresa's thinking.

'Then we must make sure the shield is held up! That's what we must do! Who knows what will happen on the battlefield? Or when exactly the Spartans will arrive? If we can give Athens any extra time at all, we must do so.

Melosa, where is this shield? Who is meant to hold it up?'

'I have it,' Melosa answered. 'I am to hide it, lightly covered by soil, in a specific place on a slope near Marathon. A fool of a slave has been instructed to find and hold it up, if we learn the Spartans are on their way earlier than expected to Athens. Once I bury the shield, my mistress wants me back in Athens to prepare for the victory celebrations.'

'Can you direct the slave so that he stays away from the shield?'

Melosa looked with growing excitement into Nyresa's face. 'I can. I can easily send him on a different route; muddle him.'

'Then we have our counter-plot,' Nyresa grinned.

'But who will hold up the shield?' Melosa asked. 'It must be someone who is prepared to hide in the slopes around Marathon for six days.'

'Why six days?' Nyresa asked.

'We don't know when the battle will actually happen. The Persians will want to fight before the Spartans arrive. But the Spartans might arrive earlier than expected. They're expected on day six. All anyone now knows is that the battle will happen some time between day one and day six. The signaller must stay hidden and be ready to raise the shield at any time during those days.' She gave Nyresa a hard look. 'The Alcmaeonidae have many spies in Athens. They will be watching for anything unusual. The person who holds up the shield must be able to disappear from his or her normal life without anyone raising the alarm.'

Nyresa's heart leapt at the chance. She yearned to undertake this task. The word 'task' rang in her memory. Of course Agariste and Rhode could not undertake it. Klio, so eye-catching, always at Gorgo's side, would be missed by her fellow musicians and, if she disappeared for six days, someone might ask where she was.

An elderly voice sounded in her memory: 'But to you, Nyresa, will fall the hardest task. Your risk will be great; much will depend upon your bravery.'

'I will do it, Melosa. I will! Rhode and I will think of an excuse to explain my absence. I will undertake this task.'

Melosa nodded. 'Then meet me tomorrow morning at the fountain in the Agora, just as the races begin. The Agora will be empty. I will tell you when and where I am taking the shield. You must go to the shield the moment the Athenian army marches to Marathon and hide there until you see the ships hovering in the bay.'

'What if Datis doesn't split his forces?' Nyresa asked.

Melosa shrugged and gave a dry laugh. 'The day Datis decides not to split his forces, Athens will be burned to the ground by evening.' She looked keenly at Nyresa. 'But I have heard the battle plans at my mistress's house. Do not be alarmed if Datis disembarks all his men and horses. The horses will need exercise and fresh water.

'There will be a great deal of talk among the generals on both sides,' she went on, 'but, believe me, the Persians are confident they can win the land battle and simultaneously take Athens on the same day. Datis will re-embark his cavalry and half his troops. Watch for the moment those ships sail!'

They rose to their feet, looking at each other. They both smiled. Nyresa suddenly wondered if her mother had looked like Melosa, and Melosa smiled to see, in Nyresa, Nyresa's mother. Melosa tapped her necklace and waved goodbye. Nyresa's smile broadened and she nodded.

4. PREPARATIONS

The next morning Nyresa hurried to the fountain in the Agora as soon as the horse races began. She knew Cherson was stablehand again and, for him, she was pleased. For herself, she was scared. She had told Rhode last night all that Melosa had said. Rhode had sent a pigeon to Agariste requesting a visit. Nyresa found Melosa waiting and anxious.

'We must be brief,' Melosa quickly said. 'My mistress expects me home soon. Listen. There are two roads to Marathon. Take the southern route, then the second turn-off to a village called Raphena. Follow the road to the beach. The bay of Marathon is just north of there. My instructions are to bury the shield on the first bluff above the beach, right near the road, at a place where four wind-bent pine trees grow. I have been told this bluff perfectly overlooks the plains and bay of Marathon. I will go in two days' time. Upon my return, I will look for you in the Agora to confirm.' Her eyes bored into Nyresa's.

Nyresa nodded. She was eerily calm inside now. She knew Melosa's words were already secure in her memory. A vivid picture of the vast sea view from the top of Thira's mountain filled her mind. Yes, she thought. Looking for a buried shield in the mountains and bluffs and beaches is not too different from trying to watch a tiny ship sail away into the sea. I will do it. Somehow I will.

Nyresa gathered the young women together as soon as Agariste managed to visit. She told them all Melosa had said in their two meetings. Klio cried. Agariste said she had to think about what she'd heard. Rhode was quiet. Soon Agariste and Klio left the house and Nyresa left to find Cherson. Sitting as still as a grave guardian, Tunnis had neither reacted nor said a word.

Rhode regarded Tunnis with concern. As Rhode's nanny, nurse and housekeeper, Tunnis had taken care of Rhode, watching over all that she did. As such, she knew every detail of the Alcmaeonid plot and Agariste's counter-plot and was well aware that Rhode and Nyresa, young girls under her authority, were deeply involved. The real danger of her girls' actions was becoming clear. The Persians were getting closer and the threat more real, and she was overwhelmed and frightened. Rhode found her by the pigeons, sitting, hands upturned in her lap, staring into space.

'The burden of this is too much for young girls, Rhode,' she said in a low voice.

Rhode gingerly pulled a slender wooden stool next to Tunnis and awkwardly sat, gently drawing Tunnis's shoulders to her. 'Tunnis, we can only worry so much, then we have to get back to our routine. If we only thought about war, we couldn't feed the pigeons,' she smiled into Tunnis's face, 'or bake sesame cakes. It's up to the gods, there is nothing we can do about it.'

'But Nyresa ... She is going off alone, who knows where, without her uncle's permission, hiding right where the battle is to take place.' Tunnis's eyes began to fill with tears.

'Yes,' Rhode nodded. 'Nyresa and you and I and everyone, we are all doing our best. You see that Athens is holding the Panathenaea, even as the Persians approach? We have to help Athens, too, Tunnis. Athens and I need you.'

Rhode's eyes beseeched Tunnis. Tunnis turned the ends of her mouth down in a brave bluster. 'I've always been by your side, Rhode, and I always will be. You know that.'

Now tears came to Rhode's eyes. 'I know, Tunnis.' Rhode hesitated then said, 'I've been thinking of what we might tell my parents to explain Nyresa's absence.' She glanced into the sad face of her aged nanny. 'I have heard from a priestess that the Eleusinium, near us, offers refuge to homeless girls.' She sighed. 'I thought we might tell my parents, when Nyresa does finally go to the shield, that she has sequestered herself at the Eleusinium to pray. My father is aware how important Demeter and Persephone are to Epiktiti and Nyresa, and I think he will accept this explanation of her absence.'

Tunnis nodded her head vigorously. Rhode took heart and smiled back. 'Now let us return to our routine. May the gods be with us.'

Tunnis grinned back, shaking her head with pride at her charge's spirit. Then she stood up to clean the cages and feed the birds.

On day three of the Panathenaea, during the feasting, Nyresa told Cherson about the shield and that she would be the signaller. He was appalled that such a task should fall to her. Again and again Nyresa pointed out there was no alternative. She insisted to his troubled face that she *wanted* to do this task. In grim exchange, Cherson told her what Miltiades had asked of him on the exercising ground. Cherson had been set a task by Miltiades, in addition to attending to his armour: during the battle he was to fight alongside Agariste's brother and cousin, never letting them out of his sight; if they tried to slip away from the battle-field, Cherson was to alert Miltiades or, if Miltiades was not near by, to kill them. The girl and boy looked at each other. The time for action had come.

After the festival last day's prize-giving, Cherson and Nyresa walked up the Mousseion to the empty Pynx which, when not holding the Assembly, they thought of as their own private meeting place.

Rumours flew about that the Persians had chosen the beach at Marathon for the battle, arriving there soon and beginning the days'-long disembarkation. The Athenians were relieved the Persians had decided against a siege of Athens. Citizens forgot their fear of and anger at Sparta and wondered if Sparta would come and help their city.

Cherson didn't know exactly when his army would be

ordered to march to Marathon. The march to Marathon from Athens took six hours. But when the battle finally began, it would be over quickly, as most such battles were – in minutes, hours at most. Nyresa knew that Melosa would take the Alcmaeonid shield to the secret spot tomorrow. One way or another, Nyresa and Cherson only had a few days left together.

As they climbed the hill towards the Pynx, Cherson, looking embarrassed, suddenly stopped, fumbling with a wrapped package he was holding. Carefully he brought out a lovely little lekythos, an oil flask, decorated with images of Artemis, hunting with bow and arrow. Helios, the sun god, was depicted over one of Artemis's shoulders and, over the other, Nyx, the god of night, with Eos, the dawn, running before her. Nyresa's smile shone upon Cherson.

'I have saved my wages from the blacksmith and bought this for my huntress, my brave, resolute Nyresa. I hear men say the ideal woman seems quiet and submissive but that, deep down, she cannot transcend her basic untamed nature. You, Nyresa, are untamed but not quiet and submissive and, as far as I'm concerned, all the better for it.'

Blushing, not from embarrassment but from the emotion of the moment, Nyresa too brought out a gift. 'Hard work earned the money for your gift. For mine to you, I have used the last of the fund my grandmother left for me, two years ago.' She held out to Cherson a similar lekythos. This one was by Sappho the painter, already famous throughout Attica. It was of a quadriga. The brilliance of the artist was shown in the horses' legs, some beautifully prancing, some pawing the ground, some elegantly planted and sturdy. Their heads and powerful necks arched backwards and forwards, drawing the viewer's eye in constant movement. The slender charioteer, loose hands lightly holding the reins, stood confident, still. Cherson and Nyresa gazed together at the image.

When they came down from the Pynx they heard the latest reports: the Persians were expected to arrive at Marathon in seven days. Cherson and Nyresa had a week before going to Marathon: he to fight the Persians, she to send them a false signal.

5. ARMING FOR BATTLE

The cry to prepare for battle had been declared in the Assembly on the Pynx and posted on the monument to the Eponymous Heroes. Every person in the city was galvanized. The men of Athens, young and old, slave and free, began preparing their armour and weaponry. Some worked over fires in the Agora or on the hill, Kolonos Agoratos, home of the blacksmiths where bronze casting-pits could be found for armourers to make breastplates or helmets or spear tips.

After parting from Nyresa, Cherson spent the dusk and evening wandering about the clusters of Athenian men preparing their armour. He knew that all adult males, whether citizens or resident foreigners or slaves, would now be known as hoplites. Each hoplite was responsible for assembling his own armour. There was no uniform armour, only the twin obligations that each man's war gear protect the wearer and instil fear in the enemy. The Persian gear was wildly different so, no matter how varied the individual hoplite's appearance, no one could mistake him for an enemy. Most hoplite helmets were terrifying, with heavy, bucket-like skull-casings, sleek cheek and neck guards, and inhuman eye-slits. Many had a large horsehair crest, which some men dyed red, decorating its fastening plates with a meandering, geometric pattern.

Cherson would be a hoplite, but it worried him that he hadn't any armour. As he walked among the soldiers, Cherson saw that he was not alone. The poorest of them had no breastplates, only leather or linen corselets. He heard them joke that the rich hoplites, with the heaviest bronze breastplates, would be the first to be knocked down and trampled. They – poor farmers covered only in leather – would be able to run (either towards or away from the enemy, someone joked). Cherson also heard many jokes about the leather flaps riveted to the bottom of the breast-plates to protect a man's private parts.

As Cherson slowly walked about the blacksmiths' fires, he noted clusters of men, presumably groups from the same region, with similar images or symbols on their shields. There were men from the four cities on the Mara-thon plain, with a black Marathonian bull displayed. Others carried shields with scorpions, anchors, lions' heads, eagles, the heads of bulls, gaming cocks, curling snakes. Even more eye-catching were shields with wild, colourful geometric patterns – diamonds and chevrons.

Cherson asked some hoplites if he could examine one

of the shields and slipped his arm through the double-grip riveted to the back. He was surprised by how heavy it was – about eight kilos. Then the hoplites brought out the spear to show him. One soldier said, 'This spear is your most important weapon. This is the hoplite's friend. We thrust and kill with it. We rarely throw it.'

'We hoplites have the best protective armour in the world,' another soldier told him. 'But we can't see much out of it, and it's hard to sit, stand or walk in. As for running, you can forget it. Full armour weighs at least thirty kilos – that's half a man's weight. *And* we're supposed to be advancing and thrusting with the spear at the same time! So . . . when the back line pushes you, as it will in just a few days, try to stay upright. Whatever you do, don't fall down. You won't be able to get up, and you'll be trampled by your own side.'

Cherson joined in the nervous laughter this speech produced. Then, as he moved along, he suddenly heard Miltiades hail him from some distance away. Looking over, he saw a pile of armour glinting in the firelight.

'Put it on,' Miltiades called, as Cherson approached.

Cherson was delighted – more than that: relieved and ready. First he slipped on the linen corselet, then drew the breastplate over his head and shimmied it down and around his torso. It latched at the side and in front, over his shoulders. Now he couldn't bend over to put on his shin-guards and so had nearly to stand on his head to get his breastplate off and start all over. He knew Miltiades would soon be teasing him. Fool, he barked at himself. He tied on the shin-guards, then picked up the breastplate again and got into it, doing it up. Then he saw the helmet on the ground.

Bursting with laughter, Miltiades came out from the shadows, picked up the helmet, the spear and the sword, and gave them all to Cherson, helmet first. Cherson avoided Miltiades's eyes and pulled the bucket-shape over his head. Now he couldn't see. He could hardly breathe. He couldn't hear clearly, though he could tell that several men's voices were surrounding him, amused at the new recruit. He thrust out his left arm for the shield and felt someone helping him. Then he opened his right hand and felt the spear shaft pressed into it. Someone tied something around his waist and he felt a sword being thrust down, beneath it.

'Now run, man!' Miltiades ordered.

Very athletic and strong, Cherson had never doubted his prowess on the battlefield. Suddenly he could hardly move. With an upward thrust he forced his legs to push and his knees to bend, willing his weight forwards, furious with himself for this clumsiness.

'Right, hoplite. You've got a few days, anyway, to perfect your advance,' commanded Miltiades, as he walked away.

Cherson suddenly was aware of an ox snorting in his ear, right behind him. He froze. Why hadn't anyone warned him? Then he realized that it was the sound of his own breathing echoing in the bronze chamber of his helmet. He tossed the shield and spear on the ground and yanked off the helmet. His face was dripping with perspiration and his ears raw from scraping against the metal plates.

If this is what it feels like at midnight, in the cold air, surrounded by my own army, without any enemy, he thought ... then what is it going to be like in the high heat of a summer's day, with thousands of Persians bearing down upon me?

6. LAST DAYS

Soon the Athenians learned what the plotters and the counter-plotters had long known: Hippias was on board one of the Persian ships. One of their own had betrayed them to the Persian empire.

Seventeen years had passed since Hippias was exiled from Athens. He was an old man now. The reforms begun just before Hippias was exiled had changed how Athens was governed, and had given each citizen a sense of belonging and loyalty. There was no going back now to the old ways of tyranny, with one man controlling the city, drawing his support from a single set of interests. Each citizen vowed resistance to Hippias.

When the news of the Persians' arrival had reached Athens, Nyresa and her friends were as caught up in the rumours and arguments as everyone else. Entrusted with questions from Agariste and impatient inquiries from Rhode, Nyresa ran out of the house to the cobbler's shop. On the way, she hailed Gorgo, who stood, as usual, at the crossroads of the Agora, spinning and coiling her new thread.

Once in the shop, she expected to find Klio – Nyresa

knew the cobbler had given Klio the key to his shop, as he had gone to prepare his armour – but she also found Cherson.

She heard Cherson's latest news. The battle would soon be upon them. The Persians had landed and were disembarking. The messengers reported six hundred Persian triremes. As for the Persian army, rumours flew wildly, but sober estimates settled on twenty-four thousand soldiers and two thousand cavalry. Datis had lined up his fleet before the beach in four rows, each of a hundred and fifty triremes. Thousands of soldiers had begun to disembark and make camp between the beach and the lake. A disembarkation of so many men and horses would take several days. The Great Marsh separated the beach from the plain where most of the fighting would take place. When the Athenians arrived, the Persians would still be disembarking.

'That is exactly what Melosa told me to expect,' Nyresa nodded, all business. 'Datis is disembarking all his men and horses. I hope to meet her tomorrow in the Agora to hear she's buried the shield.'

'Good,' Cherson replied dully.

'What's wrong?' Nyresa demanded.

Cherson spoke. 'Our top commanders have met and decided not to march until a request for help is sent to Sparta and their reply received.'

Nyresa was thunderstruck. 'Until the reply is received? How soon could that possibly be?'

Cherson shrugged his shoulders and replied, 'They've sent Pheidippides, the fastest day-runner of all Athens. He can get to Sparta by tomorrow, meet with the Spartan magistrates, and return the next day. He'll be back in three days.' He looked stonily at Nyresa. He knew what she was going to say.

'He will run one hundred and fifty miles in three days?'

Cherson nodded.

'He can't run that much in that length of time. It can't be done.'

'He can and he will,' Cherson replied. 'I was there when Miltiades asked him. Miltiades impressed upon him the seriousness of his mission, as our army will sit until he returns. He is a citizen and he knows his city's life is at stake. He is our strongest runner.'

'And Athens is to do nothing while six hours away the Persian army disembarks a force of maybe twenty-four thousand men and cavalry?' She sat down, as stunned as Klio. 'They could march on Athens tomorrow. How long can we hold out in a siege?'

'They won't. All the generals agree it will take Datis three full days to disembark. All those men need a camp with regular food, and the horses need water and exercise every day. Simply to position and anchor six hundred triremes will take time. We have three days – just. We and you will march as soon as Pheidippides returns.'

'No matter what he says?' she asked.

Cherson grew impatient. 'What do you want us to do? There are nine thousand of us. The city of Platea has sent one thousand soldiers to help us. That makes ten thousand against twenty-four thousand soldiers *and* two thousand cavalry. Two and a half Persians to one Greek. The generals thought it worthwhile to see if Sparta would join us at Marathon or block land routes to Athens, but if they don't or won't or can't, we must proceed – whatever the odds.'

Nyresa ran the next morning to the Agora to find Melosa. That day and the next would turn out to be unlike any others at the Agora. Nyresa saw huge queues outside the barber's shop. Usually the young men liked to wear their hair long because they thought it made them look more ferocious in battle (and because it cushioned their helmets a bit); it was also the fashion for men of all ages to wear full beards. But when faced with actual combat, many decided that having long hair or a beard might be a liability when fighting hand-to-hand. Hair could get caught in armour or be grabbed by the enemy.

Then there was the behaviour of the stallholders.

'Here! Take this olive oil. Here, girl!' said an old woman seller to Nyresa, the same one who had given Tunnis such a dirty look on Nyresa's first visit to the Agora. Now she wanted to give her oil for free!

Not every stallholder gave away her goods. At the jewellery table, laden with gold bracelets and earrings, bronze hairpins, portrait rings, and carved gems, the seller was calling, 'Buy gold! You can wear it, you can run with it and hide with it. It'll always have its value. Wear it, bury it, send it to family in the mountains. Gold and jewels! Buy gold and jewels here!' Nyresa glanced at the hard face of the seller, then down at the table – the prices had leapt up outrageously.

Under and around the table displaying nuts of all sorts was a mess of shells and nut meat. As she walked over, she heard the harsh laughter of a small crowd as it tipped over a table of Persian nuts and stamped on them. The stallholder wore a tight smile but Nyresa could tell she was afraid.

Nyresa bought some dried fruit and figs, but couldn't resist handing over a bit more money than required. 'Take these owls and be healthy,' she said quietly to the usually sour stallholder.

'Thank you, my dear. That's very kind. Thank you. May it go well with you, my dear.' The two exchanged quick looks of sympathy and then looked away.

Nyresa looked for Melosa at the Altar of the Twelve Gods but, though full of seated women, none was Melosa. She looked around, realizing for the first time that, apart from at the barber's shop, nearly every person she could see in the Agora was a woman. Athens would soon become a city of women, children and very old men. They would have to await their fate, not only for these three days but later too, after the army had marched to Marathon.

Then she found Melosa standing under the plane trees in the bend of the Panathenain Way. She was with Gorgo. Nyresa smiled to realize they had met, no doubt through Klio. Clearly Melosa and Gorgo had been talking. Melosa now told Nyresa that when finding a bluff high enough to signal the ships, she had had to walk along the beach from Raphena towards Marathon, further than she had expected.

Melosa smiled. 'It turns out there are many bluffs with four wind-bent pines. I'm glad I could tell you today.' She gave Nyresa a wry look. To think so much depended upon such an uncertain plan!

Nyresa returned a worried face. Inside herself she looked for courage: Athena battling the Giants, Poseidon turning back the Persian fleet and Mardonius two years ago, Demeter and Persephone speaking to her through her dreams. She felt her necklace. The gods work their ways through us, she thought. I must be brave.

Returning home, Nyresa passed the Tholos and the Bouleuterion. No one was there. Both buildings were silent. She glanced into the Tholos and saw an old man tending the fire. The emptiness was eerie and upsetting.

At home she found Agariste visiting Rhode and immediately told them what Melosa had said. They took in the information as they always did: earnestly and without comment.

Agariste nodded in understanding. 'Then you go to the shield two days from now. Take one of my pigeons with you. After you've raised the shield, watch the ships. See if they turn out to sea or land again just south of Marathon's beach. Send us word by the pigeon. I am ashamed to ask this, but please hide the shield if you can. It is shameful proof of my family's involvement.' Agariste paused for a moment, then continued, 'I've been imagining the moment you lift the shield. If the ships can see the flash off the shield, surely the two armies can as well.' She looked solemnly at Nyresa and Rhode. 'Our Greek generals will send a hoplite to find it and, assuming they succeed, the Alcmaeonid clan will be implicated.'

Rhode now spoke. 'It would be better for Nyresa to take one of my pigeons, in case it is intercepted and leads the trail back to your house. If your brother and cousin stay close to Miltiades on the battlefield, they can honestly say they had no idea who held up the shield signal.' She looked solemnly at her friend.

'I agree,' Agariste said steadily, 'though I expect they will be exiled soon after the battle. I will speak with Megacles and give him a last chance to remember his duty. If I choose my words carefully, he will not suspect that I know any more than rumours. Everyone has heard that Hippias is with the Persians and that he has allies in Athens. If Megacles suspects me, however, he may lock me up or send me to our house in the country.'

7. MOONLIGHT

During the three days Pheidippides was away, Athens held its breath, fearing a sudden Persian attack. The evening before Pheidippides's return and Nyresa's departure, Agariste sent a message for the four girls to meet at the Eleusinium, just after dark. Rhode told her parents she and Nyresa wanted to pray at the Eleusinium, while Tunnis arranged the porters and chair for Rhode. Klio got permission from Gorgo.

In the middle of the Eleusinium there was an open

courtyard with an elaborate marble basin, always clean and filled with fresh water. About this basin, each year, the young girls danced their partheneion. Agariste and Rhode both smiled to be there, together, again. The women were shy, at first, to stand in the moonlight and quietly took seats on the benches along the walls. But Agariste called them.

'Come into the moonlight, under Artemis's gaze. We have come to say goodbye to Artemis's companion, our own "nymph of the woods", Nyresa.' Agariste solemnly regarded Nyresa and again she looked to Nyresa like both her kore and the goddess Artemis.

Klio watched her three friends. These girls have become my world, she thought. Within days the doom of Athens and of us all will be known. She looked up at the moon and made a secret vow: Artemis, if you protect Nyresa and save Athens, I vow to return to Aegina, where I will make a shrine for you beside my husband's taverna. I will plant lovely flowers there and tend them, making them beautiful, every day for the rest of my life.

Rhode's porters were not allowed in the holy temple. Nyresa and Klio placed arms around Rhode and helped her walk to the courtyard's centre, while Agariste brought the chair. Once settled, Rhode found herself crying – with gladness to be out of the house with her friends, to be again in the Eleusinium, the place of her happiest childhood memory. But she was also full of fear and relief, finally to be at the awful moment of action.

Agariste felt as she imagined a marble statue might feel: centred, settled, solemn. The fate of her family and her city would soon be known. She and her friends had done what they could.

Agariste spoke. 'Artemis, under your holy light we pray. May the Spartans agree to help us and arrive in time. May our men, with the help of Athena and Poseidon, divine protectors of this city, triumph in battle. May Nyresa find the shield and raise it. And may the Persian ships see the shield and change course. All this, in your name, we pray.'

Nyresa stood, still and elegant in the moonlight, poised and serene. Her ancient, pastel beads caught the light, giving off a ghostly glow. She remembered the statue of solemn Athena, battling the Giants. She remembered the face her kore presented to mourners: not smiling but composed. She remembered her grandmother seeking from the gods to know how we are to behave in the face of threat. This is how we behave, a voice in her heart told her. This is how I choose to behave.

Her prayer rose clear and calm. 'Dear Artemis, guide me to the shield. Melosa says it is buried in the first slope, down the beach from Marathon. Give me courage to face my fear and loneliness as I wait, hiding in the hills. I choose to act, to face my fate.'

Silently the young women linked hands, creating their circle. All was silent. The stone temple's colonnade and flowering borders in the courtyard were eerily bright in the moonlight.

Then each young woman gently kissed Nyresa and departed. Alone in the courtyard she stood as still as a kore, thinking of her task, of Cherson, of her grandmother.

8. TO MARATHON

By dawn the next day, Pheidippides, that most miraculous of men, had returned as promised. The Athenian army was ready to march. On that morning Tunnis woke the girls, frantic. First she shook Nyresa awake and then ran into Rhode's room, as Nyresa stumbled out of the bed and followed her.

'Pheidippides has returned. The Spartans will come in six days. They are now in the middle of their Karneian festival and will march to us when they have completed their devotions.'

The girls stared at her. *Six days* was all each could think. Melosa had told Nyresa the Persians had set the battle date for the middle of this Spartan festival. But the Athenian army marched today. Nyresa left today. The battle would be over before the Spartans arrived.

Tunnis began to cry. 'They say he saw and spoke to Pan, on his return.' The girls watched their indomitable servant dissolve before them. Tunnis knew what this meant: the gods were now walking among men, a sign of the end for the city. She hurried out of the room in distress.

Nyresa returned to her room and quickly dressed. She came back into Rhode's room and asked which of the pigeons she should take.

Rhode's face was pale but her eyes clear. 'Take this one,' she said, pointing to a grey pigeon. 'Her name is Gethosyne, which means Joy. May she bring a joyful message when next

I see her.' Rhode and Nyresa held each other's eyes for a moment. Then Rhode smoothly caught Gethosyne and slipped her into a wicker cage. 'Here. May Athena and Artemis go with you.' Rhode turned then to feed the pigeons. Nyresa turned away, tightly gripping the wicker handle of the cage.

Just then, Tunnis returned with a sack of provisions. 'Here is food and drink enough for ten days, my little lamb. You promise me the battle will take place before six days are up?'

Wanly Nyresa smiled and nodded, tying the sack to her waist. She saw that, as scared as Tunnis was, she couldn't imagine a time when 'her girls' wouldn't need feeding. 'I'll be back on the evening of the sixth day, if not before.' Wearily she wondered yet again what would happen to her. Each step was daunting: get to Marathon, find the shield, hide, wait for the ships to reload, see them sail, raise the shield, watch to see the ships' direction, send word by pigeon, hide the shield, return home. Who knew on which day this would happen? All she could assume was that it would happen before the Spartans arrived, in six days. And some time in this period, the Battle of Marathon would take place, right below her. The odds were overwhelming that she would never see Tunnis again. She hoped the gods would forgive her lying, to reassure her dear old friend.

Nyresa and Tunnis helped Rhode down the stairs, as she deeply desired to see Nyresa off. Rhode's parents were not yet awake. After quick hugs, Nyresa hurried down the street towards the Agora. Rhode and Tunnis watched her turn the corner. For many minutes they continued standing at the door, staring at the empty corner. The streets were silent. The sound of someone approaching from the opposite direction drew their attention. They couldn't believe their eyes ... Epiktiti was walking towards them! On the eve of battle, she had returned from her pilgrimage.

Nyresa ran towards the Agora, to the cobbler's shop, to learn of her transport to Marathon. Despite being worried about his armour and going to war, the cobbler had insisted upon finding Nyresa a ride to her destination.

As she entered his shop, the cobbler spoke quickly. 'My friend, the blacksmith – Cherson's employer and land-lord – is travelling to Marathon ahead of the army. He has a horse-drawn wagon, carrying his tools for repairing armour and weaponry. His cart can't travel fast because his load is great, so he's had to set off already. Run, and you will catch him at the western gate. He is looking out for you.'

Nyresa whirled away, running as fast as she could along the south-eastern road out of Athens. Gethosyne, unable to keep a grip on her cage's bar, was tumbled along as Nyresa ran. The road went through Pallene and then along the coast and up to Marathon. The blacksmith had to be on this road, Nyresa thought. As she ran, she saw in her mind a thousand goodbye scenes enacted: aged fathers, hands raised in farewell, facing adult sons who bowed in obedience; wives pouring libations to Zeus from shallow dishes; mothers standing back, to the side, perhaps with children at their side, watching their husbands and sons don their armour and leave.

Then she saw the lumbering cart.

'Sir. Sir! I am the cobbler's friend. Please may I ride with you? Please?' she called as she ran alongside the cart.

The blacksmith called back, 'Leap in. I'm not stopping for anything. The army's right behind me. No time.' Nyresa leapt in, grabbing the back of the wooden seat, jamming the birdcage against the cart's front board and then holding it steady with her knees. She couldn't think of any way to explain herself to the blacksmith and so looked straight ahead, saying nothing. He glanced at her, then at the bird, shrugged his shoulders and drove on.

At one point he remarked, as though talking to his horses, 'I heard this morning that that festival isn't what's holding up the Spartans. They've got some internal trouble with the Messenians and have sent some of their men to put it down. That's why they aren't ready.' Nyresa didn't respond. After a while he went on, 'Maybe they're just afraid to march out of their little vale of Laconia.' Then he chuckled to himself. 'Not like our men, oh no.'

Nyresa glanced at him and nodded her head. He liked that. Whoever she was, she was tough. Doesn't say much, he thought. No matter. Not much to say.

Three hours passed. Now it was close to midday and the blacksmith pulled out some figs and bread, offering some to Nyresa, who thanked him and offered him in turn some cooked eggs and olives from her sack. He stopped the cart at Pallene to allow the horses to drink from a stream there.

'Your bird might like some water too,' he observed. Nyresa jumped slightly, out of guilt, as she had forgotten entirely about Gethosyne. She filled a little ceramic dish that was rattling around the bottom of the cage and watched Gethosyne rapidly drink from it, jerking her head up every few seconds to eye her with mad suspicion.

Before they started again the blacksmith remarked, 'See that turn-off there? The next turn-off is mine – to Marathon. The villages on the beach are Marathon, Raphena, Loutsa, and then Brauron.'

When he said Raphena, Nyresa gave a jolt, and he stopped talking and looked at her. 'What is it?' he asked.

'Raphena! That's where I'm going. I have family there. I'm worried about them.'

'Oh,' he laughed. 'Worried about them? Well, I guess so. Ten thousand men stand between your family and nearly twenty-six thousand Persians, counting cavalry. Guess you have something to worry about there.' In silence they carried on for another three hours.

'There, see that turn-off? That's to Raphena. It'll take you maybe two, three hours to get to the village.' All of a sudden his face did something so unexpected Nyresa just stared. It collapsed, not just fell, at last acknowledging the dangers ahead. 'Listen, my dear, I don't know what's to come, so I can't tell you I'll be driving back, you know? But if I'm driving back and you're at this crossroads, I will pick you up.'

Just as suddenly Nyresa felt flush with strength. Why not? She grinned a huge, confident, radiant smile. 'I'll see you here, sir. I'll be here. And you'll be here and we'll drive back to Athens.' She grabbed the wicker cage, swinging it up, over the cart's front board, and waved cheerily back at him.

His face cracked into a smile too. 'So we will. See you then, my brave girl.'

Gently swinging the cage, Nyresa trotted off down the path in the late-afternoon sun, too worried to bother about how thirsty or tired or hungry she was. She followed a path between rocky hills that, in time, became mountains. The ground itself was sandy, made up of finely ground stone and dry topsoil. She looked left and right at the mountain range through which she was passing. She could see more and more mountains behind this range, whichever way she looked. Only directly in front of her was the way clear. All the mountains were low and rounded, coming to little peaks right at the top. In the approaching dusk some slopes were bathed in a weak sun, some already in the shade. She thought they looked like waves, frozen for eternity, a choppy sea in a land of giants. She wished she could step over them in magic sandals, or fly like an eagle, or maybe sail in a magic ship.

The thought of ships brought her back to the present with a bump. Redoubling her efforts, she ran along the path through the hills. She had to climb up now and, just at the top, saw the sea and, on the beach, the village of Raphena. What had Melosa said, that afternoon in the Agora? To find a bluff high enough, she had to walk along the beach, from Raphena towards Marathon, further than she expected. Nyresa ran on.

The way to Raphena was clear now, sandy, hardly more than a path. The road left the hills and proceeded straight down to the beach on ever-flatter land. Melosa was right: there was no bluff – unless she looked behind her where she saw the beginnings of the Pendeli mountain range. Maybe when she got closer to the sea and walked up the beach she'd find a high bluff.

A very strange thing happened now. As she ran, she kept almost falling. She found she was running as though she were a rag doll. Poor Gethosyne kept hitting her head on the cage's top, then crashing to its bottom. Nyresa's knees were bending at the wrong time and she seemed to have no reliable centre of gravity. What was this? She became aware that the small pebbles on the path were running with her. The ground was alive and hopping. Overwhelmed suddenly with horror that somehow the gods were following her, coming to abduct her to take her down to the Underworld, she fell forwards and knelt on the ground, hiding her head in her arms, shaking, terrified. Then she felt the regular thud of the earth and realized that what she was hearing, feeling, was the Athenian and the Plataea armies marching, marching near her towards Marathon. Ten thousand men only a few miles away made the earth jump with every step. That meant that just around the bend, along the beach, were she to run and look, she would see six hundred triremes at anchor in the bay and thousands of Persians camped.

She scrambled to her feet and ran down the road towards Raphena and the beach.

VI

T hanks to Rhea's compromise, Demeter found a way not to kill the earth, and she returned to live in Olympus.

But first she rewarded the shepherds who had helped her find her daughter. She taught them the arts of agriculture, how to store seeds over the winter and plant them in the spring. She gave them seed corn and the wooden plough. She showed them how the plough breaks into the earth and brings forth life. And she punished Hades's gardener for revealing that Persephone had eaten the pomegranate seeds. First she tortured him, then she turned him into a short-eared owl — a bird of evil tidings, noisiest in November, just before Persephone's winter descent into the Underworld. In the end she never recovered from the terrifying loss of her daughter and her innocence, though she won her back for most of the year.

Persephone herself found little joy. Never would she become a full wife with her own family. By leaving Hades every year, she never escaped girlhood; instead she returned to her mother. Nor could she regain the innocence of childhood. Forever she would travel between her husband and her mother. Yet Persephone became a goddess. Though childless herself, each year she brings life and fruitfulness to all living creatures. Each spring, she and her mother, the goddess of fertility, embrace, rejoicing in renewal. Out of their suffering, the world is born again.

TROPHE AND NIKE

490 BC, LATE SUMMER

1. BATTLE STATIONS

Hippias stood on the deck of the commander's trireme, surveying his land, his Attica. Triremes were beached along the northern stretch of the bay and the soldiers were disembarking. He was tense. Seventeen years of expectations were now on the brink of fulfilment. But such a dream he had last night ... He had dreamt of his mother. It must be an omen. It must mean that, at last, he was in his motherland again, would regain his political power, would die of old age in Athens. His eyes circled the mountain range, swept back again over the flat, grain-filled plain, over the groves and scattered trees, and paused for more than a moment at the sight of the Great Marsh.

The waves breaking along the beach made low murmurings. It will be hot today, he thought, as he looked up at the morning sun. Holding on to the railings for support, he smiled, jowls wobbling slightly. Soon he would be with his hetaera whom he hadn't seen for nine years since their time together in Miletus. The merchant from Aegina had assured Hippias that she was as keen as ever. His bride! And at his age! Soon he would be having sea bass with the most beautiful woman in Athens.

The commander, Datis, hailed him from the shore. He raised his hand in reply. Yes, all would be well, very well.

Hippias reached out an arm to a soldier for help down the gangplank. They made their way slowly, for the planks were uneven and the surge of the waves made the whole structure shift, rise and fall. Like life, he chuckled to himself. And now I'm rising!

Once on land, Hippias straightened his back, waved the soldier away. Attica . . .

A violent sneezing and coughing fit struck him. He sneezed again and again. It must be the marathos, the wild fennel that covers this damn plain. Suddenly his whole body doubled over with the most vicious sneeze. A tooth came flying out of his mouth, landing somewhere in the sand in front of him.

Datis and the soldiers had been surprised by this extraordinary display but now, seeing no danger, laughed and congratulated him on his vigour. But Hippias was frantic. He had fallen on to his knees and was searching the sand, shouting, yelling, calling to Datis, begging for help. He seemed desperate to find his tooth. All the men near him were puzzled, and grew uneasy at his hysterical behaviour.

He could not find it. Datis, by now, was at his side and helped him to his feet. Hippias was in despair and said: 'This land is not ours, nor shall we conquer it; for the share of it that was mine – the tooth has it. It is an omen. We must depart immediately.'

Datis looked down at his feet, not trusting his face to hold the appropriate expression of seriousness or whatever it was that the old man's curious speech seemed to require. To abort the entire military operation, years in the planning, because of the loss of an old man's tooth ... It was unthinkable! It could *not* be an omen. Briskly, he ordered the disembarkation.

Hippias stood still in the sand, surveying again the mountains and the plains. He shook his head and walked over to the pine trees lining the beach.

Datis was now watching the Athenian army enter the plain from the south. Though he couldn't see further, he figured they would camp in the grove of trees known as the Herakleion, or the sanctuary of Herakles. He turned his head slightly and saw a second, smaller army marching down the plain from the northern route. The Plataeans, he thought. His spies had informed him of the joining up of these two armies, and he knew the Spartans were expected in six days' time. Once more he went over his options.

He looked at the narrow strip of plain lying between the mountains and the sea and thought again how best to position his troops. He could place his men with their backs to the mountains and have them push the Athenians into the sea. Yet that would separate his men from their ships. Even sure of victory, he felt uneasy doing that. But if his men stood with their backs to the sea, near the ships, they would have little room to manoeuvre. Yes, it was better to line up his army perpendicular to the sea, rather than facing it. He sucked at his teeth. Now what about the cavalry, his most powerful, battle-winning asset? The isolated trees dotted across the plain made deploying the cavalry risky. He searched the plain yet again. He'd wait to decide. Meanwhile, the horses must be watered, the camp drawn up. The Athenians wouldn't attack without the Spartans – that would be suicide. He had time.

Cherson marched on to the plain with head held high. He saw the sea with the six hundred battleships. He saw how the mountains enclosed the large, flat plain full of crops. He saw copses of pine trees and clusters of thick scrub. Isolated trees dotted the plain. Good. That empty flat plain would make a clear battlefield. He marched behind Agariste's brother, Megacles, and her cousin, Kallixenos, as though by chance. Soon all the men were told to make camp in the sanctuary of Herakles. Cherson kept an eye on Miltiades, who was constantly conferring with the other nine generals.

Everyone saw the ships and figured out where the Persians had to be camped. The Greek camp couldn't be seen through the Great Swamp and the pine trees that lined the far northern curve of the bay. But six hundred triremes were harder to hide, the men joked.

Miltiades strode over to Megacles and Kallixenos and, as though favouring them, requested that they camp near his tent. The two young men bowed and followed. As a matter of course, Cherson went as well for, as everyone knew, he was to attend to Miltiades's routine and battle-preparedness.

That evening, around the camp-fire of the generals, a fierce debate began. The generals in the Greek camp were divided. Half argued not to attack yet, to wait until day seven when the Spartans arrived. They were convinced that attacking without the Spartans was suicide. Aristides, a politician in peacetime and a general in war, who led this view, commanded respect. He was used, in city politics, to arguing with Themistocles, invariably taking the cautious approach while Themistocles was the more daring – and, Aristides thought, reckless. Now Aristides applied his cautious ways to the battlefield. Those who opposed him were astounded by his naivety. Did he really believe the Persians would allow the Athenians to wait for the Spartans? Miltiades led this view. He was sure the Persians would attack any day now, before the Spartans arrived, and he felt passionately that the only Greek defence was a rapid offensive; that the Greeks ought to attack first, at first light and at a running charge. As Miltiades once, a long time ago, had accompanied Darius himself on a campaign in Scythia, his experience and opinions were listened to. The generals argued late into the night.

Cherson knew Megacles and Kallixenos were listening, and that Miltiades wanted them to hear. There were games here beyond his experience. He would watch.

In the middle of the first evening of debate, a messenger arrived from Datis with a final appeal: Athens must surrender or be destroyed. If Athens surrendered now, Datis and all Persians would forgive Athens and spare the people.

The Greek generals returned no answer.

The opposing armies slept that night less than a mile apart.

Nyresa, meanwhile, had been thinking. She found a sheltered sand bluff and sat down, placing Gethosyne's cage beside her. She reviewed her situation. She had arrived at the beach near Raphena in late afternoon, and had not yet seen a distinctive cluster of wind-bent pine trees. 'It turns out there are many bluffs with four wind-bent pines,' Nyresa remembered Melosa saying. And she had warned Nyresa that she had walked quite far north along the beach from Raphena towards Marathon, before she found a bluff high enough to signal the ships.

Well, the battle would not happen now, at dusk, and it was unlikely the Persian ships would sail in the night. She still had time to find the shield.

Melosa had insisted she get to the beach between Raphena and Marathon at the same time as the Athenian soldiers marched to Marathon: the battle *could* start as early as dawn tomorrow. Though the Spartans were not expected for six days, the Athenian generals might just decide to attack early, to gain the advantage of surprise. It was unlikely – but it was a remote possibility.

Exhausted, Nyresa found a secluded spot covered by thick bushes. She reached into her food sack and found a small, wrapped bundle of honey balls. She ate one and, as always, was flooded with memories of Thira. Then she pulled off her himation and wrapped it around herself as a blanket, leaving the end to cover Gethosyne's cage. Immediately they both fell asleep.

The next morning Nyresa awoke already alert, listening for sounds of battle. All she heard were bird cries and the wind in the trees. Relieved and then aware of terrific hunger, she rolled out of her himation, stretched, greeted Gethosyne, and ate some food. Tunnis had supplied enough for a feast, she smiled to herself.

She worked her way north along the coast, up and down the sand bluffs. At last she came upon a bluff that was the start of a slope growing out of the sea and culminating in a low mountain ridge. There she saw four pine trees bent over by years of strong wind. Was this the one?

In the middle of the plateau was an area of freshly disturbed topsoil. Nyresa ran to it, brushed the soil aside – and there, to her relief, was the shield. She had found it!

But, looking left, she saw to her horror that the Marathon plain was filled with thousands of soldiers. Heart pounding, she ducked down and lay on the ground. Sliding on her belly, she edged her way off the plateau, pulling the shield after her. At the bottom, she scoured the land along the southern side of the slope, looking for somewhere to shelter. She saw a cave and ran to it. It was big enough to hide the shield, the cage and herself.

Once everything was hidden, she left the cave and, breathing hard, sat on the ground facing the sea. She pulled out more food from the sack tied at her waist and fell upon it like one of Artemis's wild animals. Cherson had teased her that men said women were wild and devious. Perhaps this is true, she thought, as she tore off a chunk of bread and hungrily devoured it.

2. POISED

The second and third days passed with no movement on either side. Both armies were ready for battle, but there had been no contact at all, no skirmishes even.

The fourth day dawned. In the Persian camp, Datis and Hippias were reviewing their strategies. Hippias had reconsidered his interpretation of the lost tooth and now felt only embarrassed by it. In part from conviction, in part to show he was made of tough material, and in part out of intense impatience, he pushed hard for battle. He could not see why the Persians hadn't attacked. They outnumbered the Greeks nearly three to one. The Greeks had no cavalry, no horses. They had no archers and no navy at Marathon. 'Why are you waiting?' Hippias stormed. 'The battle will be over within minutes.'

Datis regarded Hippias calmly. He too was sure of Persian victory against the Athenian and Plataean forces. 'I would have preferred a combined attack of infantry and cavalry.' He looked levelly at Hippias. 'You chose this plain well. Its lake provides water for the horses and the land is level for battle. The only drawback is, I can't use my cavalry. The clumps of trees make that hazardous. Having made that decision, I now delay the start of battle to be certain of our enemy's strength and numbers, and to exercise and water our horses. All this is why I chose to disembark and wait.'

Datis continued: 'I will now enact our contingency plan. As anticipated, our forces are far superior to those of the enemy. I will therefore split them in half. Half will stay here at Marathon and destroy the Athenian army. Simultaneously, the other half will sail down the coast of Attica, disembark near Raphena and, well behind the battle-field, march to Athens, easily overcoming its defenceless population. Unless, of course,' he stretched his lips into a thin smile, 'we see the signal.'

His voice swelled. 'If the shield is raised, our ships must immediately turn out to sea and sail the long way, around the Attica peninsula, to Athens. Either our victorious soldiers at Marathon will take Athens and greet our sailors, or our sailors will take Athens and greet our Marathon victors!'

Hippias beamed foolishly. Datis smiled mirthlessly at Hippias.

'Is the signal ready, Hippias?' Datis asked in an expressionless voice.

'All is ready,' Hippias boasted. 'My old family friends, the Alcmaeonidae, have thought of everything. The two gentle-men are right now in the field, masquerading as patriotic Greeks, ready to fight alongside Miltiades – while their slave is poised beside the shield, watching for our fleet.'

'That slave will know if the roads behind the battlefield are safe?' Datis pressed, threat rattling in his voice.

Hippias shifted in his seat, not used to such a tone. 'Yes, of course he will know. He will raise the shield only if there are soldiers on the roads. I have been assured, all is ready, Datis.' He thought of his hetaera, for courage. The merchant had said she was ambitious. Well, so was he.

Datis stared at him, and nodded. 'Then we split our forces now and begin the embarkation process. Today is our fourth day at Marathon; re-embarkation will take two days. On the morning of our sixth day here, half our troops sail and half attack. If the great god Ahura-Mazda is with us, on the sixth day we will have victory both here at Marathon and at Athens itself!'

Hippias nodded, pleased.

Darius was not yet finished. 'We will then be in a position to repel the Spartans,' he said. 'They will not be here before late on the sixth day – and even then will be in no condition to engage with us immediately. Nor is it likely that they will lay siege to Athens once we have taken it. No. They will return to Sparta to prepare for their own destruction. And then ... then *all* Greek cities will be begging to offer us earth and water!'

In the Athenian camp, Miltiades and the other generals watched with disbelief what they could see of the re-embarkation. Why were the Persians leaving? And without fighting? Retreat made no sense.

They kept watching. Soon it became clear that only a portion of the enemy force was departing. The Greek soldiers watched intently, warily. At the same time, Miltiades and Cherson kept a close eye on Megacles and Kallixenos, who seemed composed and even cheerful.

The Greeks had faced the Persian army for four days. Every soldier kept repeating his fear that the Spartans would not be with them until the end of the sixth day. The Persians would surely force battle before the Spartans arrived. The battle of Marathon would have to be soon. Tomorrow – or the next day.

With the battle imminent, Cherson now told Miltiades about the shield signal, carefully leaving out Agariste's connection with the plot. Miltiades listened silently and sceptically. Gossip from the servant of an hetaera and an aulos player! To a crippled daughter and niece of a metic! An hetaera's slave assigned to check the roads and warn the Persians! Women's gossip.

He dismissed Cherson and pondered this odd story of traitors of Athens. If a shield were raised as a signal, and later recovered, would it have a family design on it? He shook his head. To lead Athens into dreadful slavery demanded a dramatic motive. Suddenly the faces of Megacles and Kallixenos came into his mind: men whose family had once been the tyrants of Athens, before Hippias. No, he nearly spoke aloud. Suspicion, already in his heart, reminded him Cherson was watching those two. He had heard rumours of aged Hippias and the beautiful hetaera. In his exile from Athens, Hippias spent much time in Miletus and famously with this hetaera, then a young girl. But these were only rumours. That Hippias might have communicated with her – for nine years – through a merchant from Aegina was possible but unlikely. Still, Hippias was here at Marathon with the Persians. Hippias who had killed his brother and father. And part of the Persian force *was* re-embarking. That they were bound for Athens made sense, Miltiades had to acknowledge. And that a signal might have been arranged to warn them of ambush on the road also made sense. But . . . he shook his head in irritation. To imagine a fourteen-year-old girl hidden in those hills above them, waiting to hold up the shield, was ridiculous!

As the days of tense waiting passed, Nyresa kept her eyes glued on the Persian fleet. She observed no activity for the first three days and then watched the loading of half the ships begin on day four. To make out the ships' movements more clearly, she scrambled up the slope, keeping well down, until she had a view across the plain and the Great Marsh to the far northern beach of the bay. Often she thought of Athens, of Rhode, Agariste and Tunnis. She thought of her grandmother again and again, and wondered where she was, and when she might ever meet Gorgo and Klio. And all the time Nyresa sat, alone with her thoughts, on the sandy plateau overlooking thousands of soldiers.

As darkness fell on the fourth day, Nyresa curled up again in her himation and prayed to Artemis, thanking her for her protection and begging her to watch over Cherson in battle. She glanced at Gethosyne and thought, tomorrow or the next day everything will be decided. This was her last thought before sleep.

As the fifth day dawned, the horses of the Persians were still being loaded on to the ships. By now the divided generals in the Greek camp were barely speaking to one another. Each side insisted the other was leading the army to certain death. Tonight a decision had to be taken. Would they attack at dawn tomorrow? Or would they continue to await the Spartans, hoping against hope that the Persians would allow them one more day?

Meanwhile, all the generals watched the ships being loaded. They would soon be heading for Athens.

Miltiades rose, in that last camp-fire meeting on the fifth night, and spoke. His words were addressed to the Polemarch, Kallimachos. As the two views were evenly supported, the Polemarch had vested in him the power to cast the deciding vote. Cherson watched this tense debate and prayed that the gods would be with Kallimachos.

Miltiades spoke. 'The future of Athens lies in your hands now, Kallimachos. You can cast us down into slavery or win us our freedom – and thereby ensure that you will be remembered as long as there are people alive on this earth. Athens's position is more precarious now than it has ever been. There are two alternatives before us: submission to the Persians – and we have seen what will happen if we fall into their hands or the hands of their puppet, Hippias; or victory – which might mean we become the leading city in Greece.

'The ten generals are evenly divided between those who want immediately to engage the enemy, and those who advise against it. It is up to you to decide. But, I believe, if you give the command to attack, your country will be free and your city will dominate all of Greece. If you side with those who are disinclined to fight, the result will be slavery, for yourself and your country. Do we attack tomorrow or do we wait to be attacked?'

Kallimachos stonily regarded Miltiades. No one moved. 'We attack tomorrow!' Kallimachos declared.

3. BLOOD SACRIFICE

In the dark that next morning, the Persian forces filed south along the beach. These men were not only from Persia, but also from Lydia, Phrygia, Cappadocia, Scythia, Armenia, Assyria, Media, Babylonia, Parthia, India, Phoenicia and Egypt. They stood in twenty lines. The famous 'Immortals', the true Persians, were in the centre, next to the Scythian archers with their deadly bows. In the middle of the front line stood Datis.

The forces of Persia knew they were an extraordinary sight to behold, anticipating with pleasure the Greeks' first impression: twenty walls of shields, boldly striped in black and white, held closely together, from behind which a rain of arrows would be loosed. A forest of iron-tipped spears rose above the shields. By military tradition, the Persians wore outfits of amazing variety, of all colours, with stripes, lines, dashes, criss-crosses and dots. The more brazen and wild the decoration the better, including ribbons, diamond-leaf patterns, straight and wavy lines, and sleeves or trouser legs of opposite colours. They wore hardly any armour: leather hats with five flaps, leather tunics, leather loincloths and leather boots. Their swords, their kopis, made clear the

Persians' deadly intent: the curving iron blade, resembling a machete, an efficient two-sided hacker of flesh, hung over their shoulders, down their backs, ready.

At the base of the black sky the thinnest line of gold seeped on to the dark world. Such had been the respect for the Polemarch and his casting vote the night before, that immediately all ten generals had voted unanimously to attack at dawn. Rivals in politics and wranglers in military strategy, now they forgot all discord. When the line of battle was drawn up, Aristides's tribe placed itself between Miltiades's tribe and Themistocles's tribe: In unison the Greek generals faced their enemy. Miltiades had finally returned the Greeks' answer to Datis: total defiance.

Cherson stood on the far eastern end of the Greek line, on the right flank, directly behind Megacles and Kallixenos. They fought alongside the tribe called Aiantis, led by Kallimachos, the Polemarch, and including the famous playwright, Aeschylus. Just to their right lay the sea. The tiny waves rose, broke and gently surged up the sandy beach before slipping back down into the ocean mass. Cherson could not yet see the mountain range surrounding them, but he could smell the marathos and eucalyptus trees, the salt water and, from his fellow soldiers, sweat, old leather and fear.

As light dawned, Cherson thought again of the bloody, perilous strategy the generals had devised. He knew it from listening in Miltiades's tent. The Greeks seemed to be drawn up eight deep, and matched the Persians' front line.

However, although the front lines were of equal length, the Greek hoplites holding the centre were reduced to four deep. The tribes of Themistocles and Aristides, famed for their courage and fighting ability, were these hoplites. They faced the toughest corps of Persian soldiers, the Immortals. Cherson knew these two Greek tribes were being asked to engage with the Immortals but with the support of half the number of hoplites stationed in the flanks. The job of the two tribes was to lure the Immortals down the plain – in effect, to lose to them. As the Immortals, whooping in triumph, raced after the fleeing Greek centre section, hacking them down, the Greek flanks would shove the Persian flanks back, up the plain – into the Great Marsh.

There were two drawbacks to the plan. First, the centre section would be savagely attacked, and have no back-up. Second, the Greek flanks had to defeat the Persian flanks, had to make them flee. The Plataeans, Athens's only ally in this battle, made up the left flank, along with four of the Athenian tribes; another four Athenian tribes, including those of the generals Miltiades and Kallimachos, made up the shorter right flank. The Persian ships that were still anchored lay within reach of the Persian infantry on the Greek right flank. If the battle went according to plan, the Greek right flank would have to stop the retreating Persians from boarding those ships. Cherson stared dry-eyed at the Greeks' centre section. He saw men at their ease, ready.

Miltiades scanned the eastern horizon and saw that the Persian ships, which had been loaded over the past two days, still had not set sail. Why were they still here, waiting in the bay? His spies had told him that nearly half of Datis's troops, about ten thousand men, were embarked on the ships and that Hippias led them. He knew that all two thousand horse and their handlers were aboard. Why are they loaded with horse and men, and not sailing?

The entire cavalry is gone, he suddenly realized. *Choris Hippeis* . . . the cavalry are away, he thought. At least we will not be run to death by horses. Then Miltiades turned and looked carefully at the Pendeli mountains at the southern end of the plain. He saw nothing. No shield. No girl. The whole idea was preposterous.

Nyresa lay flat on her stomach watching the two armies. She couldn't tell Cherson or Miltiades from such a distance, though she could discern commanders from hoplites, and Persian commanders from ordinary troops. She too saw the Persian ships lolling in the bay. Today they will sail, she thought. She rolled the beads of her necklace through her fingers and remembered what her grandmother had said, that the necklace 'will protect you for all time. It has the power of Thira and of the women of Thira.'

Miltiades turned to face the men of his tribe. At the same time, Kallimachos turned to face the whole army. As Polemarch, responsible for the religious affairs of his forces, he vowed, on behalf of the Athenians, to sacrifice as many oxen to Artemis as there were barbarians killed. A goat was then brought to him. He took hold of its horns, pulling back its head, and sliced swiftly round its neck. Blood spewed forth, thick, dark, a forceful stream, a good omen. To watch, Cherson had to crane his neck, looking between the shoulders of the men in front. He could just see the spray of blood arc into the air in front of Kallimachos, forming a pool of darkness spread on the ground. He became aware of men jiggling their legs and tapping their spear shafts on the ground. They were like horses at the starting post of a race, twitching and pawing and snorting, jumpy, capable of bolting if mishandled, or backing into those behind, causing mayhem and panic. He'd seen riders trampled underfoot by white-eyed horses, frothing at the mouth.

Time to go, time to go, thought the hoplites ... You would abuse and kill my wife, enslave my children: I will kill you ... You would strike down my old father and mother: I will kill you ... I will kill you before you ever get near my home and family ... I will kill you for coming to our land to destroy our city and to burn our temples ... I will kill you for what you want to do to my brothers and sisters ...

The auloi sounded the order to march. Ten thousand Greeks rose up, shoving three hundred thousand kilos of metal and wood and leather into forward action as they marched across the plain to the rhythm of the flutes.

What am I doing on this stinking plain? thought the Persian forces. When will this campaign end? I want to go home to help harvest the crops or I'll never have enough to pay the tribute ... I hate these lousy Greeks; when I get to Athens I will take whatever gold and all the women I can get my hands on ... I will plunder their filthy temples, with their painted columns sickening against the sky ... I will get some strong Greek children as slaves for my farm ... Five months from home I have been ... I hate this stinking country ...

Datis surveyed his army. Fourteen thousand men stood at perfect attention. The thousand archers, arrows readied, rested their bows at their sides. Within a few minutes a thousand arrows would be loosed into the charging lines of the Greeks, finding their way into the hollows above their collarbones, the unprotected space over their throats and windpipes, under their arms as they held their shields and spears high, into their thighs as they ran. The Persians' shields were upright, gently set now into the ground. One quick hoist and the Greeks would face an unbroken wall of shields.

An ox was led before the Persians, a powerful white ox. Its brilliance made it look divine. Standing in front of the ox, Datis raised his curved sword high above his head, slowly turning his arm so the blade curved backwards. The iron blade glinted in the early morning sun. With a masterful stroke, he swung the blade down, slicing in a smooth curve through the front of the creature's neck, opening all its veins and arteries. So fast and true had the kill been that no blood dripped from the blade. The ox threw back its head as its body fell, front legs bending first, the massive bulk crashing after.

Satisfied that the gods had been propitiated, Datis rejoined the front line. The Persian army stood at silent attention, watching the Greeks march towards them to the shrill rhythm of the flutes.

Nyresa dusted some dirt off the shield as it lay on the soil beside her. She gazed at the curious, distinctive design of the three legs radiating from a common centre. She shook her head. This shield would certainly be recognized as the Alcmaeonid sign. She gripped the shield's back handle and braced herself to rise.

4. THE TURNING POINT

Then the Greeks did something astonishing: they started to run straight at the Persian lines. Ten thousand men, in metal and wooden armour, carrying high their twenty-pound shields, were advancing at a run. The Persian forces had joked about the scrawny farmers of Greece, scoffing at their great reputation as fighters. But now they feared for their lives; now they realized madmen were bearing down upon them. Outnumbered and unsupported by either cavalry or archers, the Athenians had to be mad to rush like this to certain death.

Cherson felt his limbs fill with strength and his heart with battle-lust. His feet and his hands surged with energy. He ran, shoulder to shoulder with his comrades, feeling their arms rise and fall with his, hearing their breath as he himself breathed. Every man wore a terrifying helmet with eerie eye-slits; their red horsehair crests shuddered with each step. Every man wore a gleaming breastplate that caught the sun.

Every man carried his shield before him and his spear in his right hand. Most had hacking swords at their sides. They ran in unison, forming the body of a single beast.

Cherson rejoiced in their power. He knew they were invincible. With the rising spirit within them no enemy could stand in their way. And then came the terrifying experience of the rain of arrows. Comrades around him began to fall, screaming. Cherson looked wildly left and right to see through his helmet's eyeholes. He saw friends on the ground yanking arrows from their necks, under their arms, from their thighs. Still the Greeks ran forwards. Cherson heard the pounding of his heart, the wheezing of his lungs, the thundering drill of thousands of feet hitting the ground; and now too the screams of pain and horror as comrades fell, wounded, trampled by those behind them. Cherson felt panic. But the beast, the running beast, held him prisoner in the front line, pressed by his comrades. All he could do was run. He could see flashes of metal and wood as the arrows whizzed past. Some hit him on the breastplate or helmet, bouncing off. Some hit his shield and stuck.

One man near Cherson received an arrow directly in his eye, straight through the eye-slit. He pulled at the arrow, shrieking, but he kept running. Blood and brains, caught on the arrow's iron tip, oozed through the eye-slit, and the man, with one last thrust, threw himself upon the Persian front line.

Nyresa lay, watching, under a spell, as though she were watching a dream. She saw the Persians: a wall of black-and-white striped shields followed by another wall, then another, then another. She saw the bright outfits and strange leather helmets of their forces. From time to time the sun glinted off a metal Persian helmet, but mostly they were much more lightly armed than the Greeks. Their spears, though, held upright and unmoving, presented a beast's back of spiked shafts, held at the ready.

The Greek soldiers made her weep; they were so brave and impressive in their bronze, crested helmets, breast-plates, shin-guards. She saw the men fall and be trampled. She heard their shrieks. She watched as the Persians lowered their spears, holding them steady at chest level as the enemy ran towards them. As though in slow motion, the Greek front line hit the Persian shafts, full on, and Nyresa gazed uncomprehendingly as the impact snapped the Persian spears. The sound cracked her heart. It was horrendous.

Cherson's chest bowed with the blow of the Persian front line. The lines collided, shield against shield. With a sound unlike any found in nature, one blow echoed a thousand times. Then came a more muffled sound, repeated many more times, of thousands of shields thumping into the backs of comrades, shoving into their bodies, ploughing them forwards into the line in front. Pressure from behind turned the front lines into human buttresses, grotesquely wielded as killing weapons, shoved directly into the spears and swords and arrows of the enemy.

Cherson raised his right arm and jabbed at the heads of the Persians, at their necks, at their unprotected chests. He had his first kill, forcing his own spear into an attacker's neck, twisting the spear so that a hole, not an arm's length away, gaped red and raw. With each thrust of his spear, he sought out soft flesh. Soon his spear was dripping blood. The line behind him thrust their spears over the shoulders of Cherson and his line: the beast was bristling with spear thrusts two and three lines deep. As each of these men pulled back his spear, Persian blood and viscera splattered over Cherson and his line.

But the Persians wielded weapons too. They slashed and cut with their machetes, slicing off Greek heads at the neck, poking into the eye-slits of Greek helmets so that men died, blinded in blood. The striped Persian shields, so gaily coloured only minutes past, were now awash with dark crimson.

Cherson was lucky to be alive. A spear was thrust directly into his breastplate but it snapped in half before it could penetrate his armour and chest. He heard this same snap repeated up and down the Persian line. Cherson was beyond panic or horror. He had become one with the war beast.

Then the Greek centre gave way ... The Persians broke through the middle of the Greek line and pursued the tribes of Themistocles and Aristides inland, down the plain, cutting down Greeks as they ran.

Nyresa braced herself against the slope behind her and pulled up the shield, sliding it against her knees, legs, and torso, to an upright position, its bottom rim still resting on the ground. She watched the ships. Those furthest out into the bay were now moving. Their sails, she saw, were beginning to catch the wind, to billow and hold, their prows slowly turning south. Three hundred triremes, choreographed perfectly, slid round to sail. Nyresa's eyes felt hot and dry. She hadn't blinked, she'd been staring so intensely at the ships. Her arms gleamed with perspiration, from exertion and terror. Her hair hung lank around her face. Watch, watch, she commanded herself. Be ready.

Miltiades, on the right flank, stepped for a moment out of time to see how his strategy – this riskiest of strategies – was faring. He saw Aristides and Themistocles, side by side, hacking and slicing man after man, even as they were being pursued. He turned to see the ships in the bay – half had slipped anchor, and were about to set sail. Horror gripped him, even though all was going according to plan and the trap was set.

He pulled his attention back to the battlefield. There was commotion at the front lines on the left flank. The Plataeans and the four Athenian tribes had turned the Persians, who were fleeing directly into the Great Marsh. Miltiades's heart soared: this was it. The *trophe,* the moment the Persians fled. The turn-around. The turning point!

5. BRIGHTLY COLOURED DOLLS

Miltiades turned his attention to his own flank. His men were forcing the Persians up the beach. On both flanks the

Greeks were in pursuit. The Persians, in terror, wheeled about, looking for a place to hide. There was no support. The strongest Persian troops were pursuing the Greek centre, and couldn't help. Those who chose to turn to face the onrush of the Greek flanks were surrounded and slaughtered. The advancing Greek flanks had joined up and caught them in a deadly noose. Those who chose to flee towards the marsh were pursued, bogged down and cut to ribbons, every one.

With their comrades being hacked to death behind them, some Persians tried to retreat to the remaining ships. The battle shifted to the bay. The fighting was fierce. Now was the time to gather the whole battle-force and hurl it at the enemy. As the Greeks ran up the beach, many later vowed they were remembering their Homer, remembering his song of the Trojan War; they felt the breath of Poseidon 'fill their hearts with strength and striking force, put spring in their limbs, their feet and fighting hands'.

Cherson was among them, Megacles and Kallixenos in his sight. He rose up in wondrous assault, killing left, right and centre. His actions inspired his comrades, who strove to match him. In this dreadful battle, Kallimachos the Polemarch fell, having fought fearlessly. His body was pierced with so many spears that it was propped upright, only the spears touching the ground.

Now. Now!

Planting her feet firmly on the slope's platform, with a grunt Nyresa raised the shield. It wobbled and fell against her. She tried to hold the side rim at the radius, but her arms couldn't stretch. Then she slid her hands down each side of the rim until she could control the shield's weight.

Turn. Turn! she ordered herself.

Slowly, to keep control, she twisted her upper body right, then slowly left, then back to right. Is the brass rim catching the sun? she cried to herself. Can the ships see the flash? She turned left, slowly right. She tried bending and straightening her knees to make the shield glint in the sunlight.

Oh, Artemis, oh, Athena, let them see the glint, let them see the flash, she prayed. May the shield flash like fire!

Miltiades surveyed the battle, on plain, marsh and sea. The ships that had slipped anchor were visible in the distance. The ships moving jarred his memory of Cherson's tale of a signaller. He turned from the battle to look at the Pendeli mountains. His eyes scanned left down to the beach, then slowly, carefully, climbed up and over to the right, searching for the signal.

And there it was. A flash on the hilltop. There, on a steep plateau overlooking the sea, something glinted in the sun, flickering, too far away to be discerned clearly, though the bronze rim of a shield might make such a glint.

The distant ships seemed to dance on the water, to sway left and right, playing with a strong breeze that had blown up suddenly. That breeze will slow their sailing, wherever they're headed, Miltiades thought. As he watched, he prayed ... For a moment the ships seemed to hesitate. Then he saw them surge out to the middle of the channel, away from the land.

Suddenly he was aware of his men around him, hoplites from his tribe, the Oineis. They too had seen this flickering. They too had seen the signal.

Miltiades turned to one of them. 'To the ships now, but as soon as the fighting has ended you must find what made that flash and bring it to me.'

Because she held the shield high up in front of her, Nyresa could not see the ships. Until she put the shield down, she would not know that they had seen the signal. She was afraid to stop twisting and turning. Finally she had to stop. Her arms and legs were shaking with the effort. In a moment she would drop the shield and break her foot or, she saw in her mind's eye, the shield would go rolling down the slope to the battle-plain. With shaking legs and hands slippery with perspiration, slowly, slowly she slid the shield back down until it rested flat on the ground. She raised her eyes to the ships. They were going out to sea.

She turned to the battlefield. She saw the left flank turn the Persians back, pursuing them into the swamp, and the right flank burst up the beach, breaking the Persian left flank. Now the running and the screams and the clashing of armour and the ripping of flesh became real to her. She watched as again and again hoplites hacked and hewed – and were thrust at and pummelled in turn. All about the plain were corpses of Persians, like brightly coloured dolls strewn across the floor. Sick with sorrow and fatigue, still she watched, mesmerized. Then she began to move. She gave herself orders: hide the shield; get Gethosyne; write the message and release her; run to the crossroads. Efficiently, coolly, she began to follow her own orders. She scraped away the dirt first loosened by Melosa. Laying the shield flat, she covered it completely, gently packing down the soil. She then slipped down the slope, got the bird, and wrote with charcoal on a strip of linen: SUCCESS. SHIPS NOT LANDING. SAILING. She wrapped the message round Gethosyne's ankle and tossed her, in a smooth movement, into the air. Gethosyne found her bearings and flew off, flapping deeply, soon soaring west over the hills. With powerful grace she found the air current within the winds and rode upon it. May Artemis watch over you, Nyresa prayed.

Meanwhile, as the Persians fled towards their still-anchored ships, Cherson and his comrades cut them down. The best Persian troops, the Immortals and the Scythians who had pursued the Greek centre, were fleeing towards the ships. Exhausted, the last Persians now faced the Greeks' right flank. They fought well and held the Greeks back while others of their comrades clambered on board. Nine thousand Persians escaped, thanks to the bravery of these men. Datis was among those who escaped. Seven ships were captured; the rest, crammed with injured and bewildered survivors, limped out to sea.

Finally the killing was over.

*

The victorious Greeks – Athenians and Plataeans – gathered that noon at the trophe, the turning point. They sprawled on the ground, bloodied and exultant. The ratio of dead was twenty-five Persians to one Greek. A mere one hundred and ninety-two Athenians had died in battle; to four thousand nine hundred Persians slain. The hoplites were silent, awed by the enormity of their victory. Although many gods were praised, Athena's name was on every man's lips. She had come to the rescue of her city. The one hundred and ninety-two martyrs had died in her service. Almost immediately a trophe was to be erected on the spot in the plain where the Persians were turned around. It would be a tall, elegant column, with an Ionic capital.

It was while fleeing to their ships that most Persians had been cut down. As they fled, their unprotected backs had been easy game for the hoplites. They had been slaughtered in their thousands.

Pheidippides was sent to Athens to bring news of their great victory. With victory secure, Miltiades addressed his men.

Before the gathering, he had asked Cherson to join them. Megacles and Kallixenos sat with the Oineis tribe, too. Rumours had circulated throughout the Greek forces that, only minutes ago, a shield used as a signal to the Persians had been retrieved from a slope of the Pendeli mountains. The shield, brought to Miltiades's tent, bore the triskeles of the Alcmaeonidae. Megacles and Kallixenos, who had fought courageously and continuously all morning, swore they knew nothing about it. They were outraged at the suggestion of treachery. Had they not proved themselves today? they demanded.

Then Miltiades addressed the tribe. 'While we were fighting, nearly half the Persian forces and their cavalry set sail for Athens.'

The one thousand men of the tribe stared at their general blankly.

Miltiades continued. 'As we expected, the Spartans do not depart for Athens until tomorrow. They plan to come immediately to Marathon, to honour the fallen and make offerings to the gods.' He looked at the men. He watched his men calculating. Each man was working out the risks that now faced his wife and family: Spartans were marching in the direction of the city, Persians were sailing towards it. Sparta, Athens's enemy for generations, now came as friend. Just last year Sparta conquered Aegina, right at Athens's door. No, the Athenians understood that their city's alliance with Sparta was complex and unreliable.

'I know I have your full support in our decision to march back immediately to Athens.' Miltiades kept watching his men, not laying out for them the inadmissible threat of a Spartan presence in Athens. 'We will be there to receive our Spartan allies,' he said, 'and together, the two armies will greet the Persians.' Then, rapidly, he changed his tone.

'You have fought as heroes today,' Miltiades proclaimed. 'You have won a rare victory, with the help of Athena and Poseidon, Theseus and Zeus. Apollo and Artemis also attended us. Dionysus was among us in our battle-frenzy, and Pan. We shall never forget our run through the rain of arrows. We shall never forget the courage of our centre as it lured the best of the Persian soldiers down the plain. We shall never forget the turning point, given us by our allies, the Plataeans, and four of our tribes. We have lost a great leader, Kallimachos, Polemarch of our army and acting general of the Aiantis tribe. He fought most bravely and won renown. When we return to Athens and the city is finally safe, we will find a way to honour and remember them.'

Now, before all the tribe, after this extraordinary day, Miltiades turned to Cherson, praised his bravery and called him Ajax, likening him to the founder of their clan. His uncle was acknowledging his lineage, enabling him to claim his public name. Of course, the men of Miltiades's tribe had heard much gossip about Cherson's heritage, and they congratulated him. Miltiades glanced at Megacles and Kallixenos, but said nothing. Many men saw the glance and interpreted it correctly: the matter of the shield would be raised in Athens, on the Pynx.

Miltiades turned again to the troops and gave the order to ready their departure. A gust of wind ruffled his beard and blew his tunic about his legs. 'In six hours we will be home, ready to receive the Spartans. We will have time to rest before facing the Persians. Let us march with all speed to defend our city. The south wind will not slow *us* down. This day is ours, and ours the future.'

6. TO ATHENS

Nyresa ran along the road in the noonday sun. Soon she passed the turn-off to Raphena and was travelling along the main road towards Athens. When she came to a little stream she paused to drink and rest, to catch her breath. As she sat a moment, in tall grass by the stream, she heard the creaking of a wooden cart. The blacksmith!

'WE WON,' he shouted to her. 'We won. We won, we won, we won!' His face was so creased and cracked with smiles and joy it was almost distorted. 'It was a miracle. Athena was with us!'

Standing by the cart, grinning back, she nodded.

'Oh, if you had seen it,' he exclaimed. 'Our men rushed them! Took them completely by surprise. Our bronze-armoured hoplites ran a mile across the plain and, in perfect formation, killed them! Then we tricked them. Our centre dropped back, luring those "Immortals" to follow them down the plain, and then our wings surrounded them. What a fight! Jump in. Hurry,' he commanded. 'The Persians who escaped, including Datis and Hippias, pushed out to sea. Everyone figures they're all headed for Athens. They should arrive there tomorrow night.'

The blacksmith looked at her while he slapped the reins on the horses' rumps. The cart jerked forwards. 'You look different somehow ... older. And where's your bird?'

Nyresa could only grin with joy. She was thinking,

Gethosyne – JOY – was exactly the right bird to send to Rhode!

'You never did talk much, did you?' he chuckled.

The blacksmith's cart was nearly empty of the heavy metals he had brought to the battlefield, so they made good time. The blacksmith kept talking to himself, working out his speed and the distance, but Nyresa could tell it would be all right; they would stay well ahead of the army. She wouldn't think about the Persians sailing towards Athens.

After what seemed an eternity, their cart rounded the cut in the mountain and they saw Athens – beautiful, silent in the distance. Nyresa saw a tear roll down the blacksmith's cheek, as he looked on his home. As their cart approached the gymnasium exercise grounds where the army was to camp, they saw the temple with the grand bronze statue of Herakles holding his bow and arrow. The sacred grove of olives promised respite from the heat of the plains.

As Nyresa bade goodbye to the blacksmith, she looked back to see the Greek army rounding the very bend which had given them their first view of the city. Even from so far away, she could see the army break formation. Nyresa grinned as she saw the men hugging and dancing and tossing their helmets into the air.

7. PARTHENOS

The women, children and old men watched Pheidippides run the dusty road across the plain from the mountains to

Athens. His news was their fate. Panting, staggering, he climbed the last steps up the slope to the base of the Acropolis. Thousands stood in absolute silence, looking at him, waiting. Old hands were clenched. 'VICTORY!' he cried, and sank to the ground, dead of exhaustion.

As the army gathered at the Herakleion, the generals sent messengers down to the Agora to post the lists of those killed in battle. Before celebrating, each family went to the monument to see whether the name of a relative was there. News spread quickly of how few names there were, so that almost immediately upon the army's arrival there was dancing and shouting in the streets. Only around the postings of the Leontis tribe and the Antiochis tribe were most citizens solemn. Soon they would cloak their grief with the rich robes of honour and pride; their sons, husbands and brothers were the martyrs who saved the city. Thanks to those who died, the Persians were not now in possession of Athens. The city was not burned, the sanctuaries not desecrated, the men not killed, and the women and children not abused. Democracy was alive, the Assembly would meet again on the Pynx, the court would continue to hold jurisdiction over trials, every citizen would have his say in government, and all Cleisthenes's reforms would stand. Athens was still free.

Rhode insisted to her parents and the newly returned Epiktiti that they and Tunnis take her to see the lists, carried by her porters. Rhode's mother was flustered by the request.

'My dear, why must we go? We have not lost anybody and would just be in the way of others who need to see the lists. Besides,' she added, looking away, 'the Agora will be so crowded and noisy. Really, wouldn't it be just as good to celebrate here?'

'Rhode is right,' Kleomenes countered. 'We know so little of what has happened to deliver Athens. The Agora is the only place to find out. No doubt we will meet up with Nyresa there too, just released from her sequestration at the Eleusinium – unless she goes home first?' he ended, glancing for confirmation at Epiktiti.

Epiktiti spoke. 'Go, please. I will wait here for Nyresa.'

Kleomenes nodded to Epiktiti and then looked steadily at his wife, who sighed deeply again, and raised one arm, indicating to Tunnis that she wanted her himation. Tunnis and Rhode exchanged quick looks, and soon the group was heading for the Agora.

Meanwhile Nyresa had quickly sought out Miltiades's tribe, where she would find Cherson. That he might not have survived was unthinkable, yet she could not see him. She watched until she began to lose hope. Then there was a figure walking towards her. Tall, slim, tired looking, Cherson held open his arms and Nyresa ran to him. Neither spoke for a long time.

She pulled herself away and smiled broadly at him, and he at her. Without words, they walked towards the olive grove.

Once under the trees, Cherson suddenly grew serious.

He turned away from her to speak. While listening, she raised her arms to her head and began plaiting her long, black hair. She gazed solemnly at him, and her lips curved in the faintest smile.

'Nyresa,' he paused, but still kept his face turned away. 'Miltiades honoured and recognized me at the trophe after the battle.' He turned back, saying, 'He has brought me into his clan and his tribe. He will seek confirmation from the Assembly as soon as it meets.'

He grew still. Nyresa had woven her hair into the one long braid of a parthenos. He caught his breath. 'You would have me, Nyresa?'

She nodded, happiness filling her face.

His face became wild as joy warred with fear. 'Am I not too young? Will your grandmother approve me so soon after …' His voiced choked. He had been alone, with no money, and of the lowest status for years. Now in one day the gods had granted him everything. He feared the enormity of his good fortune.

'Shush,' she said and, placing her hands on his shoulders, tilted her face and slowly stretched to kiss his lips. 'Shush,' she smiled as he pulled her towards him and, seizing her head in his hand, pressed her face to his, kissing her again and again, on her lips, eyes and neck.

As the moon sailed through the sky, they dared to dream about the future. Cherson's training and military service lay ahead, but then so did so much else. With the Persians gone and Cherson's name made, anything was possible.

Then they parted; Cherson to tend to military duties,

Nyresa to her home. When she arrived, breathless, she threw open the house door and bolted up the wooden stairs, expecting to find Rhode and Tunnis. Instead she found her grandmother waiting for her.

After the longest of embraces and many tears, Epiktiti explained that she'd arrived just after Nyresa's departure, that Rhode had told her everything about the plot and their counter-plot. Epiktiti was amazed by her granddaughter's courage and determination.

'You have grown up, my little Nyresa,' she said. 'And I am proud of you.'

Nyresa smiled happily. She noted, though, that Epiktiti said nothing about her parthenos plait or Cherson. Perhaps Rhode had not told her about him.

Then Epiktiti's voice changed, growing solemn. 'Do you remember our talk, by your kore on Thira, Nyresa? There I told you I needed signs from our gods, to know if they gave their consent to the Persian occupation. Is Ahura-Mazda more powerful than Zeus? I wanted to ask the gods how we were to behave in the face of the Persian threat.'

Nyresa nodded, remembering the plain at Marathon littered with dead Persians, the boldly striped, colourful out-fits bloody and ripped. The only way the Athenians could have won was by divine help. Athena and Apollo were on the battlefield, Poseidon on the sea; surely the gods had spoken.

Epiktiti looked and smiled into her granddaughter's eyes. 'The gods answered me, but not as I had expected.

They called me to travel, to pray and reflect. By going on this pilgrimage, I enacted the gods' will. By your raising the shield, you enacted the gods' will. In my absence you discovered the gods' wisdom.'

Nyresa looked back, puzzled.

'The power of the gods is revealed to us in dreams, oracles, earthquakes. But it is also revealed to us through our capacity to think and to do what is right. You, Nyresa, found the link between the Agora and the Alcmaeonid plot; you encouraged Klio to take heart; you touched poor Melosa's heart; alone, you took on the task of the shield and stayed upon that slope until the ships moved; you raised the shield, sent Gethosyne, and returned home safely. These were all your accomplishments. But also the work of the gods, of the gods working within you.'

Nyresa nodded slowly, pleased and proud to be praised so. But now the image of Cherson crowded her thoughts and she knew she had to tell her grandmother about him.

'He is young to be a husband,' was Epiktiti's first response. 'In Athens and on Thira men marry at twice the age of their wives. Your cousin mentioned this young man to me, and I have worried about his family and how you would live.' Nyresa blushed. 'I could not let you marry a boy with no family, Nyresa. But now you tell me that his uncle has acknowledged and honoured him. And you, my lovely granddaughter, should have been a parthenos last year – you are old enough to marry. If you are sure in your heart that this is what you want, I give you my consent.'

Nyresa's face was wreathed in smiles and the two embraced. 'I was afraid, Grandmother, that I was doing wrong to encourage him without your consent.'

'It seems you did a lot without my consent,' her grandmother laughed, but then she nodded and grew serious. 'It was, indeed, immodest of you to walk with him alone and to exchange gifts. Many would disapprove. Things would have been different had I been here. But remember, my darling,' she smiled again, smoothing back Nyresa's hair as she used to do, 'had you not spent so much time in the Agora and become so close to Cherson and Klio, you couldn't have helped Agariste and Rhode unravel the Alcmaeonid plot. The shield might not have been raised.' She looked solemnly at her granddaughter. 'Athens might have fallen to the Persians, had the Persian men and horses disembarked just south of Marathon.' She looked off into the middle distance. 'Our gods knew all this, Nyresa.'

It took a little while for Rhode and her family to make their way through the Agora to the monument. There was a crush of people at the notice boards and Kleomenes ordered the porters to place Rhode back behind the cluster of plane trees adjacent to the monument. Tunnis pressed forwards to look for Cherson's name, not sure where to find it, as he was not, as far as she knew, a member of any of the ten tribes. She couldn't find it anywhere and returned to Rhode, crying with relief.

Rhode, seeing tears running down Tunnis's face, nearly fainted. When Tunnis reported what she'd seen, Rhode collapsed back into her chair, released from worry. Tunnis then ran off to see her friends and hear their news, and to try to find word of Nyresa. Rhode gazed up at the stars and wondered, mutely, what the constellations foretold.

Klio and Gorgo were also at the monument. Klio was searching intently, looking for Cherson's and the cobbler's names. Gorgo stood back in the shadows, waiting. Neither man's name appeared. Klio was suddenly aware of someone close to her. She turned in some alarm and saw Melosa, less than a hand's breadth from her, yet shrinking into the shadows.

'Melosa!'

'Shush,' Melosa cautioned, hardly making a sound.

Klio quickly realized what danger Melosa was in – or about to be in. Tunnis had run to the cobbler's shop earlier that day, to tell Klio and Gorgo that Gethosyne had returned with the glad message. Klio had then told Melosa. The Persian triremes were due to arrive tomorrow night, which seemed ages away. Was the Alcmaeonid clan under suspicion? Had anyone linked them to Melosa's mistress? No, Klio thought, this is too much to unravel so soon. Concerned and inquiring, she turned her huge brown eyes on to Melosa.

'Say nothing, Klio,' Melosa warned. 'No one yet suspects, but the trail will lead to my mistress's door eventually. I am leaving Athens.'

'I hadn't realized that the consequences would be so grave for you, Melosa,' Klio murmured. Melosa stared hard at Klio and Klio realized that her eyes were shining and her face radiant. Melosa was happy!

'I am not going because I'm afraid, Klio. This is what I want. So many memories were revived by Nyresa.' She smiled warmly. 'I want to return to Thira, Klio. I want to go home. If Athens is free, Thira will also remain free. Because the Persians have been foiled, I am able to choose to sail home. Please, say goodbye to Nyresa for me. Thank her for her courage. Tell her she is a true woman of Thira!'

'You are both true women of Thira,' Klio nearly sang, hugging her friend.

Melosa then pulled away a little. 'And you, Klio? What will you do?' she asked most gently.

'Me? I too am going home.' But then she immediately lowered her voice. 'I vowed the night at the Eleusinium that if the Athenians won, I would return immediately to Aegina, marry my fiancé, and create a shrine and garden to Artemis which I would tend all my days. And Gorgo is coming with me.'

The two happy women quietly said goodbye and Melosa slipped away into the crowd. As Klio watched her disappear, she caught sight of Rhode, sitting amid the plane trees behind the monument. She made her way across the Agora through the crush of people.

Rhode pulled herself more upright, delighted to see her friend. Rhode beamed into the lovely, solemn face before her.

Klio whispered, 'I have just spoken to Melosa –'

'How was she? Surely there is real danger for her

here if they ever find out what she did,' Rhode whispered.

'There's no need to worry. She is joyous. She is returning to Thira.' The two young women looked silently at each other.

'That is just as well,' Rhode quietly responded. 'She was very brave at a terrible time. For years she has been caught between the Greek and the Persian worlds. I hope she will find calm now in her homeland.'

Klio frowned and studied her friend. 'Rhode,' she began hesitantly, 'I too am leaving. Gorgo and I are moving within days to Aegina. I vowed, our evening at the Eleusinium, that I would return there and create a shrine for Artemis, if she would help the Athenians win.' She looked earnestly at Rhode. 'What will you do now?' she asked her, quietly and slowly.

All the sadness in Rhode's heart overwhelmed her. It was not for Melosa that she felt awash with sorrow; it was for herself. 'You're going to leave, Klio?' she asked. Before Klio or Rhode could say more, Gorgo emerged from the darkness and stood before the two young women. Rhode looked up at the dignified blind woman.

'Klio, is this Nyresa's cousin?' Gorgo asked in a low, thrilling voice.

'Yes, Gorgo.' Then Klio turned to Rhode. 'This is Gorgo, my guardian.' Klio smiled. Rhode did not know what to say in the presence of the magical old woman. She knew, of course, that this was the Fate of the Agora, who had guided and comforted Nyresa.

Gorgo turned her sightless eyes towards Rhode. 'Klio

226

has asked what you will do now, Rhode. Have you an answer?' Rhode felt that Gorgo was looking straight into her heart. She felt she had to speak the truth, to this woman she had never met.

'I do not know what I can do. I have thought much about the Eleusinium where I had been so happy as a child,' Rhode began slowly. 'I would like to be a priestess there,' she whispered, looking fully into the face before her. 'In time I fear I will not be able to walk at all, but I would like to oversee the teaching of the partheneion.' She smiled.

Suddenly Rhode's parents broke into the small circle.

'Excuse me, I am Kadoma, Rhode's mother,' Rhode's mother said to Gorgo. 'I don't believe we've met.' Kadoma started with surprise and unease upon noticing the unseeing eyes of Gorgo. Kleomenes, who knew of Gorgo, hoped to be introduced to the beautiful Klio. However, neither the flute player nor her guardian turned their attention from Rhode.

Gorgo continued: 'You will be welcomed there, Rhode. The Eleusinium honours women touched by the Fates.' Gently Gorgo smoothed her old, thin hand along Rhode's legs. Rhode stiffened but did not pull them away; her mother looked outraged. 'They understand such women have been chosen,' said Gorgo. 'Only chosen women are allowed to enter into the life of Demeter's sanctuaries, in Athens and in Eleusis, to wear the white robe, and to carry the key. You will be respected and valued.'

'Kleomenes, do you know this woman?' Kadoma demanded of her husband. Not receiving an answer quickly enough, she turned to Gorgo. 'I believe this is enough talk about my daughter's future, thank you. Tunnis? Where is Tunnis? Kleomenes, please! Find Tunnis and tell her to instruct the porters; we will return home now.'

Kleomenes, disliking any scene, turned to Rhode and said, 'Daughter, what is all this business about the Eleusinium and white robes?'

Rhode's upturned face still glowed from Gorgo's words. 'Father, I wish more than anything to serve in the Eleusinium in Athens. I will be near our home but I will have my own life.' She looked up at him as he stood above her chair. Her mother looked disbelieving. Tunnis, who had appeared alongside her, started to cry. Rhode quickly added, 'Tunnis, you must stay to look after my parents, but visit me each day and tell me how you all are. You can convey messages between us.'

Through her tears, Tunnis smiled. Kleomenes glanced at his wife, who looked outraged and bewildered. He smiled gamely at Rhode. They understood each other. He nodded.

'I give my approval, daughter,' he said. Then, pulling himself up as tall as he could, he announced, 'And now we must find Nyresa!'

Evening had come and the Agora was now lit by countless fires casting flickering light on exultant people. Kleomenes looked around, hoping to spot his niece among the crowds.

Suddenly Nyresa emerged from the throng, grinning, dazzling, her hair plaited as a parthenos. Epiktiti was behind her. Rhode saw Nyresa first and cried out in happiness.

8. DAWN

In an open balcony in the palace of Susa, Darius stood facing the great plains and mountains of his land. Words from the messenger from Marathon echoed in his mind. He envisaged the battle and saw his poorly armoured men facing the bronze of the Athenians.

'The Athenians are our inferiors,' he thundered into the vast space before him. 'We outnumbered them. We had cavalry, they did not. We had ships, they did not. We chose the battle site.' Sneering, he went on, 'We had Hippias to guide us. And in Athens a rebellion was prepared, ready to spring.'

Little flickers of pain shot through his chest and left arm, and then through his shoulder and up his neck. Darius frowned and shook his shoulders. He turned his head right and left, and raised his chin. The pains came again, more quickly. He started to cross one arm over his chest but stopped himself. He was Darius. He did not show pain. He sat down on the throne to overlook his empire, as far as the eye could see.

He placed both hands on the chair arms to show his strength. Each wooden chair arm ended in the carved head of a bull. His hands gripped the bull heads and he was reassured. Still frowning, he looked off into the distance. A statue came to mind. A glorious statue of a lion attacking, killing a bull, sinking its jaws into the bull's back. He gazed inwardly at the statue. The bull's body had collapsed. It was dying and its expression was filled with pain. The lion was so real Darius could feel it. He could feel its teeth bite down into his own back. The pains started again, whipping through the old emperor's chest and back and stomach.

'We cannot lose,' he shouted, crossing his right arm over his chest to hold in the pain. Letting go completely of the chair, he now crossed his left arm over his right and rocked in torment at the pressure on his chest.

He bellowed: 'We will return and demolish them, obliterate them all. We will destroy Athens as though it never existed! We will ruin Sparta, Corinth, Argos!' The pressure intensified. 'Thebes, Mycenae, Olympia, Delphi!' He spat out 'Delphi' as though the name were poison, his face purple with rage and pain.

Slowly his fingers found the throne's two bull heads. 'We will have our revenge!'

9. THE MORROW

There were celebrations all the next day. Everyone danced and sang and feasted. The Spartan advance party, the 'flying-column', arrived around midday. They were two thousand in number, and three thousand more would arrive the next day. But they would not be needed. The Persian triremes sailed into Phaleron at dusk, but left when they realized both the Athenian and the Spartan armies were guarding Athens. Clearly Hippias and the Persian commanders were not willing to engage the combined Greek forces. Victory had come to Athens. Already people were talking of a temple to Nike, goddess of victory, on the Acropolis.

Epiktiti had taken Nyresa to the Eleusinium to talk privately. They sat on the benches in the cool courtyard. Nyresa, dazed with happiness, saw that her grandmother was solemn. Nyresa grew attentive.

Epiktiti paused, as if thinking deeply. 'I have brought you here, to the shrine to Demeter, to tell you what I have learned in prayer to this goddess. Nyresa, I have learned the secret of your nightmares.'

The old, wise, kind eyes looked down into the girl's intense face. 'In your dreams you are not the one falling, Nyresa, you are not Persephone. The dreams that have tormented you are about what happened to your mother, not you. It is your mother who married Hades – forever.'

Nyresa sat still in amazement.

'You felt her loss so keenly that you took on her life and died, in your dreams, for her. Always you cried for your Demeter: how sad that you cried in my arms, in the arms of your mother's mother.

'You were born out of sorrow, but you lived and grew. You have become a real woman. I understood how I was like Demeter when I prayed at Eleusis; and then, when I stayed at Brauron, I saw how Artemis had been protecting you. You see, Artemis protects young girls, especially in their growth from childhood to maturity. Artemis is the goddess of maidens and does not always approve romance and marriage. But she does stand by young women in childbirth.

231

Nyresa, she has been watching over you during your child-hood. I am convinced she was by my daughter, comforting her as she gave birth to you, and that she took you over to raise and protect after my daughter's death. Did you not confide in me that your kore, in the cemetery on the hill on Thira, had the face of Artemis?'

Now Nyresa saw the wonder and truth of her grand-mother's words: she was meant to live, meant to marry and have children. She gave thanks to Artemis for her protec-tion and, while mourning her mother, no longer feared she would share her fate.

They rose and walked to the stone basin in the court-yard's centre. Dipping her fingers in the cool water, Epiktiti touched Nyresa's forehead and lips, leaving glimmering marks on the girl's face.

Much later that evening, after all the celebrating, Agariste brought her eight-year-old son to the Acropolis. They walked in silence up the marble stairs and through the ancient portico. Hand in hand, they passed between the ancient temple of Athena on their left and the unfinished temple on their right. The little boy gazed again at the huge statues in the pediments of the ancient temple. He saw the two lions attacking and killing the bull. And on another side, he saw Herakles fighting the Hydra. Inside the temple, Athena sat still and serene, in her golden diadem and gold cloak. Agariste and her son bowed, and offered prayers to the goddess who had delivered them.

As they walked out and between the temples again, the

little boy craned his neck to look at the unfinished temple. Its white marble columns stood stark but beautiful in the moonlight.

'Mother?' he began, 'I think there should be a bigger temple here.'

'Bigger even than this one will be?' she asked, smiling.

'Yes,' he answered solemnly.

'Why?' she asked.

'To thank Athena for saving Athens.'

Agariste nodded. 'What would you have on it?'

The boy gazed at the unfinished temple. 'The festival. When we all walk through the city and give Athena her new cloak. That would be good. She can be on the front with the cloak and the girl weavers. The other gods can be there too.'

'But what about yesterday's battle? How can the temple show that?' his mother asked.

The boy thought. 'Horses. The hoplites who died can be riding horses all around the sides. Everything can be flying: the horses' manes and feet, and the men's heads turning this way and that!' His eyes shone at the vision.

'But we had no cavalry at the battle,' she gently reminded him. 'Only infantry, only foot soldiers.'

'Oh, I know that. But they're heroes. Heroes live on after death in the Elysian Fields. They'd be riding their horses to the Elysian Fields.' The boy was mesmerized, caught in the spell of his imagination. Agariste gazed at the temple, seeing his vision with him.

'Come, son,' his mother then said. 'Come to the wall here. Look out over the city with me. Tell me what you see.'

They walked together to the side and both leaned on the wall, gazing over the city, lovely in the moonlight. Dawn was breaking.

'Athens, mother. The wonder of the Ages.'

Agariste's face was solemn as she gazed over the city, now bathed in the pink light of dawn. She thought of her brother and cousin, who, so far, had escaped accusation. She thought for a moment of her uncle Cleisthenes. Then she wrapped her arm around the little shoulder of Pericles. Eos, a new dawn, she thought. A new day.

Nyresa lay in bed, too happy to sleep. She had refused to undo her parthenos braid, which felt like rope beneath her back. Her eyes shone in the pale light. So much had happened she could not begin to review it. The future was too exciting even to contemplate. She smiled in the dark. She found herself remembering the flight of Miron, soaring over the Acropolis and heading south to Thira. She flew with him, over the sea and the islands, until he came to Thira. She saw him soar over the kore near her mother's grave. She imagined leaning against the sun-warmed kore's stone skirt. As the warmth spread through her, so did the love of her mother and Artemis. Nyresa turned to look out over the vast blue sea where the dolphins swam and the ships left white trails. She dreamed of sunny days, warm breezes, flourishing crops, and laughing children.

POWER AND STONE
Alice Leader

130 AD. Britain is a conquered land – the edge of civilization.

It is a long, long way from home to Hadrian's Wall – and Marcus isn't sure he wants to be in cold, gloomy Britain. He and his brother have come to be with their soldier father, here at the edge of empire.

Bran is a local boy who wants to be friends – but his sister is wary of the Romans. Is it really possible to be friends with your conqueror? As dangerous tensions build, the two families are about to find out . . .

'Maybe the past is not another country' – *Guardian*

'A vivid picture of life in Roman Britain emerges in Alice Leader's excellent debut novel . . . [she] packs in a huge amount of fascinating detail' – *FT*

'Leader's blend of the supernatural with historical detail is excellent' – *Independent on Sunday*

BLOOD RED HORSE
K. M. Grant

You need three things to become a brave and noble knight:
A warhorse. A fair maiden.
A just cause.

Will has a horse – a small chestnut stallion with a white blaze on his brow. Ellie is a fair maiden – but she's supposed to marry Will's older brother, Gavin. And as for the cause, King Richard is calling for a Crusade. The Knights of England must go to the Holy Land to fight.

Will and Gavin will go. Blood will be shed. Lives will be wasted. But through it all, two things will be constant – Ellie, and a blood-red horse called Hosanna . . .

'This really is unputdownable, featuring great characters, plenty of action and some unforgettable moments. This new author is definitely one to watch' – *Bookseller*

TELL THE MOON TO COME OUT
Joan Lingard

1939. Spain is a country torn apart by civil war.

Nick has come from Scotland in search of his father – who left the family home three years ago to fight in Spain. He never came back.

Spain is a dangerous place for a boy with no identity papers. Nick has been told to trust no one. But then, ill and desperate, he meets Isabel, the daughter of a sergeant in the dreaded Civil Guard. She offers him help. But can he trust her?

'Deftly mixing adventure, history and romance, Lingard tells the story of this sometimes forgotten war with great sensitivity and sureness of touch' – *Scotsman*

Read more in Puffin

For complete information about books available from Puffin – and Penguin – and how to
order them, contact us at the appropriate address below. Please note that for copyright
reasons the selection of books varies from country to country.

www.puffin.co.uk

In the United Kingdom: Please write to Dept EP, Penguin Books Ltd,
Bath Road, Harmondsworth, West Drayton, Middlesex UB7 ODA

In the United States: Please write to Penguin Group (USA), Inc. P.O. Box 12289,
Dept B, Newark, New Jersey 07101–5289 or call 1–800–788–6262

In Canada: Please write to Penguin Books Canada Ltd,
10 Alcorn Avenue, Suite 300, Toronto, Ontario M4V 3B2

In Australia: Please write to Penguin Books Australia Ltd,
250 Camberwell Road, Camberwell, Victoria 3124

In New Zealand: Please write to Penguin Group (NZ),
Private Bag 102902, North Shore Mail Centre, Auckland 10

In India: Please write to Penguin Books India Pvt Ltd,
11 Panscheel Shopping Centre, Panscheel Park, New Delhi 110 017

In the Netherlands: Please write to Penguin Books Netherlands bv,
Postbus 3507, NL–1001 AH Amsterdam

In Germany: Please write to Penguin Books Deutschland GmbH,
Metzlerstrasse 26, 60594 Frankfurt am Main

In Spain: Please write to Penguin Books S. A., Bravo Murillo 19,
1° B, 28015 Madrid

In Italy: Please write to Penguin Italia s.r.l.,
Via Felice Casati 20, I–20124 Milano

In France: Please write to Penguin France S. A.,
17 rue Lejeune, F–31000 Toulouse

In Japan: Please write to Penguin Books Japan, Ishikiribashi Building,
2–5–4, Suido, Bunkyo-ku, Tokyo 112

In South Africa: Please write to Longman Penguin Southern Africa (Pty) Ltd,
Private Bag X08, Bertsham 2013